Nin

Trace Richards

Twisted River Press
Louisiana, Missouri

This is a work of fiction. All the characters and events portrayed in this book are either products of the author's imagination or are used fictitiously.

Revised Edition: 2016

First Published by Twisted River Press, LLC in January 2011
Twisted River Press
Louisiana, MO 63353
www.Twistedriverproductions.com

"Shadow of Perseverance"
2016

ISBN: 978-0-9828218-2-4

Printed in the United States of America

Acknowledgements:

The author would like to thank Steve Condon of the Louisiana Missouri Police Department for answering any questions that he had regarding police procedure and investigation, as well as Stephen K. Hayes and James Norris of the SKH Quest Center for their time and guidance in Taijutsu training.

Trace would also Like to thank his wife for her ever constant encouragement, his mother for helping him get the laptop that this work was written on, and the friends and family that offered their support throughout the making of this book.

Author's Notes:

This book is a work of fiction. While the city of Elmira, NY is a real place, it is represented fictitiously with modifications made to some locales as needed. Although some factual information exists regarding ninja history within these pages, embellishments have also been made regarding their combat arts for similar reasons. For those interested in seeking to pursue the authentic history and martial ways of the ninja, I recommend contacting the Bujinkan, Genbukan, Jinenkan, and/or SKH Quest organizations.

"Ninja aspired to merge their spirit and techniques into one, and become 'uncommon' common people. Some people did try to become 'superhuman' through their training in Ninpo, but they did not achieve great success as Ninja. It is quite easy to become a superman; Ninjutsu makes one aware of just how difficult it is to become a 'normal' human being."

-Way of the Ninja: Secret Techniques
Massaki Hatsumi

忍

Nin

Prologue

The youth nervously glanced around while quickening his pace. All around him was silent. The occasional scuffing of his white sneakers across the earth was the only sound heard as he made his way through the wooded area, the trees and night were working as one to make his journey as discreet as possible.

Almost there...

After the passing of several more seconds, his stride came to a startled halt. A hoarse voice that was all too familiar called to him. "Hello there Justin," The youth turned to face his rear in response to hearing his name. "You got the money?"

Justin cast a few more glances around the area before returning his gaze to the man who now stood before him. A dirty brown long coat hid much of his form as long, tangled strands of greasy black hair hung over his shoulders. "Yeah... Yeah I got it."

The man began to advance. Slowly, he sent his right hand into the confines of his coat to extract something from within. Justin's eyes widened greedily as the man stopped before him. His hand remained veiled in the coat as his icy eyes stared down at the wiry youth. "Money first." he coldly reminded.

Justin flinched at the tone of the man's voice as he reached for the back pocket of his jeans. With a trembling right hand, he opened his wallet, the ripping sound of the Velcro cutting the stillness of the night air. The man watched as Justin produced a fifty-dollar bill. The man in turn removed his hand from beneath his coat, exposing a small plastic bag which contained a white, powdery substance. The pusher's lips took the shape of a wry grin once the exchange had been made. "Pleasure doing business with ya kid."

Suddenly, Justin's eyes began to widen, a look of fright in them as he gazed not at the pusher, but into the trees beyond.

"What?"

A puzzled look formed on the pusher's gruff face as he turned, seeing nothing in the small, wooded area but shadows. Turning to face Justin once again, he saw only the youth's back. Taking off in a full sprint, Justin's feet pounded the earth as he ran with all the speed that he could muster.

As the pusher watched Justin's retreat in perplexity, the sound of something sharp slicing through the air echoed in his right ear, a stinging sensation beneath it to follow. He cried out in pain and surprise as he felt something begin to trickle down the edge of his jaw. Quickly he grasped at the area in response, seeing his fingers stained crimson upon the removal of his hand. "What the fuck?"

The pusher turned to face his rear once more. Cautiously, he scanned the area, seconds passing as he saw and heard nothing. A burst of movement to his left suddenly grabbed his attention, a dark silhouette seen out of the corner of his eye that was soon lost amid the trees as he quickly turned in hopes of spotting whatever was amiss.

In panic's grasp, he withdrew a hefty colt revolver from beneath his coat. He aimed the gun with a very unsteady right hand while simultaneously scanning the darkness ahead of him. Seconds passed as he heard only his own nervous breathing.

Within a few moments, a shadowy figure emerged from behind one of the trees at his right. The being's movements were fluid and seamless while stepping eerily into view. Quickly the pusher turned to fire his weapon in response.

The dark figure darted behind the trees at once. The explosive sound of two shots fired from the revolver blasted the still night air.

Swiftly the figure bolted. The pusher spun, firing four more shots as the being's movement's encircled him. His eyes widened in terror as the sharp clicking sound of the gun's hammer indicated an empty cylinder. The figure had merged once more with the surrounding darkness, unhindered by the gunfire.

Deafening silence filled the air once more. The pusher's heart raced. Cries of fright erupted from him as he turned to flee toward the perceived safety of the nearby city's lights, pure fear spurring him to escape whatever, or whoever was lurking in the dark.

Chapter 1

The soft blue eyes of the young woman scanned the front page of the newspaper that she held before her, the text at its top boldly proclaiming it to be the *Elmira Star*. While utilizing one of the arm rests of the sofa in which she reclined for back support, her blue denim clad legs extended the length of the couch's seat; the right leg resting atop the left to cross at the ankles as her toes slightly flexed beneath socks of navy blue cotton. Without taking her eyes off the paper's text, she casually extended her left hand toward a steaming cup of coffee that set atop a small rectangular table positioned in front of her seat.

Cautiously, she sipped at the hot beverage with a slurping sound before returning the white ceramic mug back to its resting place beside her. Without warning, a large pampered looking orange tabby cat leaped onto the sofa. Its purring was reminiscent to a miniature car motor as it made its way from the woman's feet. Rubbing its head against hers, it pushed its nose through the lengthy strands of her straight flame red hair. Her lips formed into a soft smile as she gently stroked the feline from head to tail, its back arching with each pass before it settled to rest beside her. The coloration of its soft fur was barely a contrast to the white t-shirt that she wore as it soon went to sleep.

"Good night Buster..."

Returning her attention back to the newspaper once more, her eyebrows furrowed as she read the front page's bold headline and accompanying article.

Unexpected Death Hinders Medicine Man Investigation. By Clayton Drake

Elmira NY- Authorities efforts to apprehend the drug lord known only as The Medicine Man were dealt a serious blow, with the sudden death of Robert Kane. Kane, who was arrested for possession and distribution of an illegal substance, was found dead during the early hours of the morning in his cell at the Elmira Police Department. Sources estimate the time of death was between 1 and 3 am. According to sources in the Elmira P.D., Kane had information which was vital to...

The sudden ringing of a cordless telephone at the young woman's rear snatched her attention away from the newspaper article. With a sigh, she turned her slender form toward a small circular end table at her back. Reaching over her left shoulder with her hand to retrieve the receiver, she answered the call after the second ring.

"Hello?"

"Detective Devins?"

Slowly she sat upright.

"Yes, this is she..."

"This is Officer Kenneth of the Elmira Police Department. Someone reported gunshots in or near Sutherton Park. We picked up a teenager not too far from there on Franklin Street... the kid had cocaine on him."

"Alright, I'll be there in a few minutes."

忍

The headlights of the white Crown Victorian pierced the night. The car's approach slowed to a stop at the curb to park amid others of a like make and model, an absence of police lights separating the unmarked vehicle from the rest of Elmira Police Department's squad cars. Detective Jessica Devins emerged from her vehicle and approached the crime scene with a confident stride. Almost hypnotic flashes of red and blue from the emergency lights filled the area. Jessica produced her badge from beneath her denim jacket to gain clearance.

"So what exactly happened here?" She asked aloud, reattaching the badge to her belt while awaiting a reply from any of several nearby officers.

From amid the trees nearby, a plump black man approached. His rotund form was clad in the blue shirt and black pants of a police issue uniform, the buttons on his shirt straining tightly against his bulging mid-section.

"Well, we aren't quite sure yet Detective." He replied, his friendly voice rising in befuddlement. "We've found several places where bullets hit. Seems that a handgun of high caliber was the weapon, but who or where the shooter is has yet to be determined."

"What about the kid picked up on Franklin Street?" Jessica asked, glancing about.

"We're guessing that he was fleeing the scene." The plump officer responded. "He's at the station right now, but we don't think he was the shooter's target."

"You don't?" Jessica's eyebrows raised in confusion, her gaze settling back on the officer in front of her.

"It's real strange, Detective." he continued. "From the circumference of the shots fired, we've determined their point of origin to be right here." He gestured to the area on the ground, now taped off with yellow barrier marks.

"I'll find out what the kid knows." Jessica said.

As she moved amid the greenery to leave the crime scene, Jessica's keen eyes suddenly caught sight of something peculiar within her peripheral vision. Her curiosity seized, she turned to spot something sticking out of a nearby tree. Quickly acquiring a pair of latex gloves and an evidence bag from forensics personal, she moved closer to investigate.

Twigs snapped beneath her dark navy sneakers as she made her way to the object of her curiosity. Her eyes narrowed on arrival, the veil of distance parting to clearly reveal the object she sought. Deeply embedded in the tree was a flat plate of metal.

Curiously, she examined her find while sheathing her hands in latex. Seemingly made of some type of steel, she estimated the plate's diameter to be roughly that of her hand's palm. Its diamond like shape resembled that of a four pointed star, edges between the points curving slightly inward toward a square shaped hole located within its center. Cautious of the plate's razor sharp edges, she extracted it from the tree, a dull thunk reverberating from the trunk upon its removal. She placed the plate of metal into an evidence bag and sealed it carefully as she walked away, unaware of the dark figure concealed in the branches above that silently watched her every move.

忍

Jessica calmly entered the interrogation room. Closing the door behind her, she placed a thin manila folder in her possession to rest on the square metal table at the room's center. Taking a seat in a straight-backed metal chair, she scanned the folders contents. Several seconds quietly passed, except for the flip of another page from the folder. The youth seated directly across from her glanced nervously around at the white walls, his gaze coming to meet that of his own reflection in the one-way mirror at his left, other officers watching him unseen from behind it.

"Justin Cadwell..." Jessica finally said while continuing to read the file.

Startled, the youth jerked in his seat as she slowly raised her head, bringing her eyes to bear on him.

"I'm Detective Devins, Narcotics Division..."

Jessica examined Justin with intense eyes while allowing her words to further unsettle him. With dull bloodshot eyes, the dark haired teen stared back warily, his scrawny frame lacking the mass to fill his green t-shirt. Clearly the use of illegal substances had taken their toll on his body, with one guess being as good as any as to how long he had been poisoning himself.

"I understand you were found in the possession of cocaine." Jessica stated. "Care to tell me where you got it from?" Justin averted his eyes, casting his gaze to his worn white sneakers. Jessica's eyebrows furrowed, the youth's silence beginning to erode her patience. "I don't think the answer to my question is on this floor, Justin."

"I don't know, okay?!" He snapped as he looked up, a frantic look in his eyes.

"You don't know?!" Jessica repeated as her ire began to rise.

"You're gonna have to come up with a hell of a lot better than that..."

Several more seconds passed in silence, as Justin's eyes began to well up with tears. Jessica used the time to calm herself before continuing the interrogation.

"I'm gonna ask you once more, Justin. Who provided you with the coke?"

"I don't know his name." Justin replied sullenly, his voice quaking slightly as he fought back tears while returning his gaze to the floor.

Jessica's facial expression softened slightly. Deciding to approach the interrogation with a bit less intensity, she mentally noted that a male suspect had supplied Justin with the drugs.

"There was gunfire at the scene Justin." Jessica started "Was he shooting at you?"

"No." Justin answered, looking up from the floor again. "There was someone else there."

Jessica raised an eyebrow.

"Someone else?"

"Yeah, someone else was there, in the dark."

"Did you get a good look at them?" she asked.

"No. It was too dark." Justin repeated while shaking his head.

Jessica released a sigh that hinted at exasperation. She leaned forward while closing the folder.

"Listen Justin, I'm going to be as forthcoming as I can be with you." she started, pausing briefly to let her words sink in before continuing. "We need to know who provided you with the Cocaine, and it would be in your best interest to cooperate with us. By law, you can serve for up to five years in prison for possession of an illegal substance. That's something you might want to take into consideration since you will be turning eighteen in a couple more years, after which you can and will be tried as an adult."

Justin rubbed his eyes with the back of his hand to wipe away tears, sniffling as Jessica continued. "That notwithstanding, you're probably gonna spend some time in Juvenile hall. Helping us might help your situation here though. So, what do you say Justin?"

"Okay." Justin sniffled after a few moments of silence. "What... what do you want?"

Jessica's eyes softened, her lips forming into a slight smile at the boy's willingness to cooperate and help in the investigation.

"You said you didn't know the name of the man who sold you the cocaine. Do you think you could provide a description of him?"

Still avoiding eye contact for the most part, Justin nodded.

"Yeah, yeah...I guess so."

Jessica's grin widened.

"Good, I'll send someone in to get you to a sketch artist for a rendering."

With that she stood in preparation for her departure, collecting the manila folder she had brought with her. "Your parents have been notified and are waiting outside for you." she said before taking her leave.

忍

The headlights of coming and going vehicles combined their efforts with those of street lamps on the bridge's sides to ward off the night. Jessica's vehicle glided inconspicuously amid the others. Traversing the spans known to Elmira's close to forty-thousand residents as the Walnut St. Bridge.

Briefly taking her eyes off the road, she glanced casually at the calm waters of the equally familiar Chemung River that flowed beneath to divide the city. Returning her gaze to the road ahead, she began to think back to times past.

Originally from the small town of Bath, Jessica Devins' family moved to the much larger city of Elmira shortly after she had turned 8 years old, with her father seeking more opportunities for advancement in his career of law enforcement. Steeped in the Civil War's history and strife, Elmira served as a prison camp during these times, with P.O.W.s giving the city the label of "Hellmira". Today, the city stood as something of a tourist attraction, serving as the burial place of Samuel Clemens, otherwise known as Mark Twain, famed author of *The Adventures of Huckleberry Finn*.

Growing up, Jessica had always been something of a tomboy, tending to favor the clothing and activities of the opposite gender over dresses and dolls. In school she was a straight 'A' student, and was involved in many of Southside High's extracurricular activities, excelling particularly well in athletic pursuits such as basketball and volleyball. In particular, she enjoyed martial arts, having been a practitioner of Wing Chun Kung Fu since she was twelve years old.

Later in life, her ambitions to follow in her father's footsteps with a career in law enforcement came as little surprise to her parents. Soon after graduating high school, she joined the Elmira Police Academy, rising to the upper echelon of her class fairly quickly.

Tragedy however, struck the young cadet shortly after her graduation from the academy. After being shot during an attempted drug bust, her father's near twenty years as a police officer ended with his death in the line of duty.

Through the anguish that came with her father's demise, Jessica struggled on. Driven by a carefully honed anger, few on the force could match her tenacity, as she made collar after collar in her crusade to keep society's evils off the streets. Within eight months' time, she would advance to become a detective of Elmira Police Departments Narcotics Division; the death of her father being something that she never fully recovered from even with the passage of much time.

Now at the age of thirty, she faced her greatest challenge to date, one who had been eluding authorities for nearly five years, the drug lord known only as The Medicine Man. Speculations abounded as to who the enigmatic criminal was. Only Robert Kane appeared to have this knowledge, and it went to the grave with him as he was found dead in his cell. Medical experts later claimed that a stroke had been responsible for the middle aged man's untimely end.

Jessica's mind snapped back to the task of driving home once more. The sound of a car's horn blared angrily behind her as she suddenly realized that she had been stationary at a green light for several seconds. Sighing, she pushed the accelerator pedal to resume her journey while casting a brief glance to the car's passenger's seat, the manila folder that contained her own copies of the Medicine Man case file laying upon it. Returning her eyes to the road ahead, she drove on, her mind again drifting to other matters as she pondered the flat star shaped plate of steel that she had found, and its potential connection to the Medicine Man case.

Chapter 2

The city pulsed with activity, its citizens moving about in their private endeavors. The chilly air that accompanied still early spring nights encouraged the men and women, traveling along the sidewalks, to dress accordingly in their comings and goings. The sounds of vehicles on the streets echoed all around them. Unseen by all, above the hustle and bustle, a dark figure glided along the rooftops.

Lithe powerful legs propelled the mysterious black clad figure. Only a determined pair of walnut brown eyes showed from behind a mask that was comprised of two black strips of cloth, tied and intertwined at the back of his head. Onward he sprinted, crossing from one roof to another with seemingly effortless leaps. Stopping suddenly in a crouching position, the masked figure slowly stood to look out at the sights and sounds of the city spread out below him.

Discreetness, such as this, always brought to mind the memories of his apprenticeship in the rare skills he now possessed, and how he came to acquire them. His work in a past career sent him to the island nation of Japan, where he met an extraordinary man; a master of an almost forgotten martial tradition. Immediately ensnared in the net of intrigue, he humbly requested guidance and teachings.

For nearly a decade, he resided in Japan while the master shared this knowledge, knowledge that was only passed on to those with the most honest and sincere of intentions. Rigorously he trained in these ways of warfare, working to master formidable martial arts skills which utilized the entire body as a weapon, along with a plethora of strange combat tools and weapons. Methods of movement that permitted him to tread silently over any surface were honed to perfection, as well as the ability to move about unseen, strike from the shadows, and then vanish again. At the end of his apprenticeship, he returned to his homeland of America as a skilled warrior in the art of invisibility, the way of the Ninja.

It was with these skills that he would pursue his self-appointed mission, the down-fall of the Medicine Man. The faceless drug lord had been flooding Elmira's streets with his poisons and influence for nearly half a decade now, half a decade too long. It was time for the corruption to end.

Upon hearing the sound of a police car's siren below, he resumed a crouching position. In silent poise, he watched as the familiar vehicle sped past his position on the roof of what was once an old drug store. He knew well that the police now possessed evidence of his involvement with the night's disturbance, and although he was certain that his lost weapon could not be linked to his true identity, he decided regardless, that his quest would be best served to continue on another night. Slowly standing again, he dashed off once more, his form disappearing into the night.

Chapter 3

The blaring of an alarm ended the stillness. Slowly, Jessica's eyes opened. Her right hand groggily emerged from the tangle of white sheets to cease the annoying sound as she pressed the stop button atop the nearby clock. With sleepy eyes, she gazed at the clock's face, eight A.M. easily spotted in bright green digital numbers. She pushed herself up to a seated position in an attempt to throw off the clinging remnants of sleep, her bare feet coming to rest upon the tan carpet of her bedroom floor, its soft fibers gently tickling her soles.

Still somewhat groggy, she stood with a yawn. Taking a moment to stretch her arms and back, she made her way across the bedroom to her nearby bathroom, the white satin gown that she wore flowing slightly with her stride. Stopping and kneeling by the bathtub, she twisted the hot and cold knobs of the tub's faucet. The sound of pouring water echoed off the tubs interior as she checked the temperature of the stream with her hand. After a few minor adjustments to ensure comfort, she lifted the faucets stop to send the stream gushing out from the shower head above her.

Within moments, she stood and disrobed. Her gown landed upon the powder white tile of the floor in a crumpled heap as she stepped into the tub and pulled the shower curtain closed.

The impact of the rushing water was instantly revitalizing as Jessica lowered her head into the stream, allowing the water to wash over her hair. For several seconds she stayed this way before throwing her head back, the soaked strands of her hair flung back with the motion as water streamed down her athletic frame to collect in a continuous puddle at her feet. After finishing her shower, she dressed and grabbed a quick breakfast in the form of a toasted bagel, before stepping out the door of her home.

Jessica exited her vehicle once parked, her pace quickening as she made her way toward the Elmira Police Department. Serving also as City Hall, the tall building of earthen brick boldly stood against the bright blue sky, with a pointed four-faced clock tower serving as an apex atop a senate style roof of oxidized green metal. The barred windows of its cross-beamed base seemed to watch her approach as though they were eyes. Pausing briefly, she cast her gaze up toward the sculpted motif of an eagle with the face of St. Michael staring out resolutely from behind it. Returning her eyes to the path before her once more, she made her way past the Greco-Roman pillars of the building to its entrance.

With a shove, Jessica sent the double doors of the building inward as she strode inside. Walking with a purpose, she crossed the black and white diamond tiled floor. Moving along walls of gray, she passed by many metal desks and coworkers, several greetings exchanged before she arrived at her own. A folded newspaper lay atop its surface, her attention grabbed by the front page's bold headline.

Local Philanthropist Makes Generous Donation to Police Department

Under the headline was a photo of an elderly man who stood with the police chief. Between them, they each held the end of a check in one hand while their free hands were clasped together in a handshake. Jessica grinned slightly.

Rolland Sinclair. She knew little of the man, having only seen him briefly in his comings and goings within the department, as he occasionally spoke to the police chief behind the closed doors of his office, presumably about donations, fundraisers, and other such charitable happenings.

Taking her seat, Jessica sat the newspaper aside and began sorting the various paperwork on her desk. Suddenly, the falling of a faint shadow upon the top of her desk snagged her attention.

Standing in front of her was one of her fellow officers, a tall slender man who grinned warmly while extending his hand to offer her a sheet of paper.

"Good morning Jessica." Jessica smiled in return while taking the paper from him. "Good morning Rodger. What's this?"

"It's the artist rendering you requested last night." Officer Rodger Benning replied.

Jessica examined the sketch, committing to memory the gruff looking visage of the drawing in the event she ever encountered anyone that was similar in appearance.

"Unsavory looking fella." she commented with a grin. Her eyes remained on the rendition of the suspect as she continued. "Do we have an APB out on him?"

"Yeah, but we haven't found anyone matching the description yet."

Jessica raised her gaze to Rodger once more. "What about that metal plate I found at the scene?"

Rodger shifted his position to seat himself on a bare corner of her desk, a slight chuckle rising from him. "Oh, you mean your ninja star?" he asked.

Jessica frowned in slight annoyance at the attempt to rib her, with Rodger soon after resuming a more serious attitude toward the topic at hand.

"Well, your find seems to have been home made." He continued. "Thing was clean... not a print on it. We've checked several different martial arts surplus stores, and none sell anything quite like what you found. We're still looking into other avenues for purchases of steel in small quantities, for someone to make something like it. The thing is in evidence though if you need it."

Jessica nodded. "Thanks Rodger, keep me posted."

"Sure thing. We'll let you know if anything new turns up."

With that Rodger stood once more, taking his leave as Jessica set about the task of completing her paperwork.

Chapter 4

The yellowish glow emanating from a halogen bulb served as the only source of light in the dark, trash strewn alleyway. Within the small, lighted area of a side doorway, a group of men, five in number, stood. Smoke streamed from lit cigarettes, forming a billowing haze about the group as they conversed amongst themselves in hushed tones.

"You guys hear about that shit that went down at Sutherton Park last night?"

"I heard Thomas went ape shit and started shooting up the place."

"Yeah, claims he saw some boogey-man or some shit."

"Where is he anyway?"

"Yeah really, that fucker is ten minutes late."

The sound of approaching footsteps suddenly grabbed their attention. All five of them turned in unison to face whoever was coming. The silhouette of a long coat clad individual drew nearer, with long stringy hair and gruff facial features becoming fully visible once the newcomer entered the light.

"About fucking time you showed up Thomas."

Thomas reached into one of his coat pockets and pulled out his last cigarette from a crumpled package. With unsteady hands, he stuck the cigarette into his mouth and lit it, calming down after several drags.

"Sorry." He solemnly replied, while peering over his shoulder in a paranoid manner.

"What the fuck is with you man?"

"Yeah, what happened last night?"

Thomas took another lengthy drag from his cigarette. "Listen," he said to emphasize his need for attention before continuing. "Someone attacked me last night."

"Was it the boogeyman?"

A chorus of chuckles resounded from the group. Thomas' eyebrows furrowed in frustration.

"Look at my face god-fucking-damn-it!" he snapped, pointing to the laceration in the right side of his jaw. "This is fucking serious!"

The group once more grew quiet, giving Thomas their full attention.

"Okay, what happened?"

"Who attacked you?"

Thomas finished his cigarette, tossing the butt aside before continuing his story.

"I don't know who it was. I never got a good look at the fucker. It was like he could just disappear."

"What do you mean "disappear"?"

"It was crazy shit. Like he'd just step into the shadows and he'd vanish into thin air. He was like..." There was a moment of silence as Thomas searched for the right words. "like a ninja out of the movies or some shit."

The other five men burst into fits of laughter.

"I'm being serious!" he yelled in protest. "I shot at this fucker six times and I didn't hit shit! I don't even know how he did this!" Thomas pointed again to the cut on his jaw, the laughter of his colleagues continuing.

Suddenly, the halogen bulb above the group exploded. Abruptly, their laughter ceased as they were plunged into darkness, their bodies showered with shards of glass as they scrambled about in blind desperation.

"What the fuck!"

Through dazzled eyes, Thomas was able to make out a shadowy silhouette emerging from the darkness of the alleyway beyond. His eyes opened wide in horror as the one he knew to be his attacker from the previous night closed in fast. Desperately, he fumbled for the gun beneath his long coat. Stumbling a few steps backward, he drew the weapon and quickly took aim.

With great celerity the being moved, disappearing into the mass of flailing silhouettes. A sense of uncertainty clawed at Thomas, stopping him from firing for fear of hitting one of his own allies in the ensuing bedlam.

Oh fuck!

Thomas suddenly felt an intense stinging sensation in his wrist as he was somehow struck below the base of the thumb. Crying out in as much surprise as pain, he lost his grip on the gun. A creeping numbness ascended his arm as his weapon clattered to the pavement, lost in the chaos. Again crying out, he turned and bolted, fleeing the scene as quickly as he could. His heart pounded as he ran from the alleyway. The sounds of agonized screams and battered flesh filled the night as those he left behind fell. All was soon silent again as a black clad hand claimed from the pavement a star shaped plate of steel, leaving behind the remnants of the halogen bulb that it had shattered.

The shadows of the parked car's interior blanketed Jessica as she sat in silence, the only sounds around her to be those of other vehicles that occasionally passed in the night. Rare was the moment that she was able to enjoy such serenity, and with the peace and quiet, she could relax as she casually feasted on a ham and cheese sandwich that would serve as her dinner for the night. Each bite of the sandwich was slowly chewed in an attempt to savor the taste, with a feeling of contentment taking hold of her as several minutes passed in this manner.

Without warning, the police band radio in her car came to life, chasing away the tranquility as it called her to duty.

"Attention... A disturbance was reported in an alley at Water Street. All units in the vicinity respond immediately."

An exasperated sigh escaped Jessica as she laid her sandwich aside to answer the call.

"Rodger that. Detective Devins responding. Ten-four."

She activated the emergency light on her car's dashboard before racing to the scene.

So much for peace and quiet...

The unmarked police car sped along the city streets, other vehicles in her vicinity yielding right of way to the detective as she urgently raced passed. Within a matter of minutes, she had reached her destination, the first to arrive at the scene. Directing her car to the side of the street, she exited its cab.

Listening carefully, her ears caught the sound of painful moans emanating from an alleyway a few feet ahead. Quickly arming herself with a long flashlight of black metal, she readied her service pistol while cautiously approaching the alley's entrance. Slowly she peered into the darkness, aiming the flashlight's beam ahead to light her way.

Her eyes widened in shock as she entered the alleyway, the flashlight's beam revealing what seemed to be the end result of the disturbance that she had come to investigate. Five men lay scattered about. Grimacing in pain, they all held twisted fetal positions as they favored various parts of their seemingly injured bodies. "My God..." Jessica whispered to herself. The groans continued, soon to be joined by approaching police sirens.

Two more officers arrived on the scene.

"Detective Devins, what happened here?"

"Get an ambulance fast!" Jessica ordered urgently, whirling around to face the other officers who quickly dashed off at her plea to summon medical assistance.

Returning her gaze to the scene, she slowly moved about, carefully stepping over and around the battered men while aiming her flashlight about to scan the area. Suddenly, her eyes narrowed the beam of her flashlight landing upon a prone revolver that lay isolated from the battered men near a wall to her right. Holstering her own firearm, she made her way toward her discovery for closer examination.

She carefully lifted the weapon, using a tissue extracted from the inside pocket of her jacket as a cautionary measure against ruining any fingerprints. Holding the weapon between her first two fingers and thumb, she silently studied the revolver in the flashlight's beam as one of the other two officers on the scene approached her rear.

"Paramedics are on the way."

Jessica gave no reply as she stared down the dismal alleyway, into the darkness beyond.

Jessica hurried through the frenzied activities of the other officers en route to her desk. Quickly taking her seat upon arrival, she opened a file folder that she possessed and began scanning its contents.

"Quite an exciting night, eh Detective?" A voice proclaimed, drawing her attention from her work.

Looking up toward the plump, black man in police uniform, she returned the smile that he gave her while resting her arms upon the desk.

"Yeah Walter, to say the least. It turns out those bullets that you guys found at Sutherton Park last night trace back to the gun that I found tonight. My hunch is that whoever that gun belonged to is also the one who sold the cocaine to that teen. I'm not sure what happened last night at Sutherton or in that alley way tonight, but I think that once we've checked the revolver for prints, we may be on our way to getting some answers."

"The revolver is being run for prints as we speak." Officer Walter Briggs replied, his mouth shaping into a proud grin.

Closing the file, Jessica leaned back in her chair, crossing her right leg over her left in a relaxed manner.

"What about the five men we picked up tonight?"

"Oh, this is really gonna bake your noodle Detective." Walter replied with a slight chuckle.

Jessica' lips shaped into a slight grin as she clasped her hands in her lap.

"Don't keep me in suspense, Walter."

"Well, we've got enough to put them away. Guns, drugs, you name it and they had it. The hospital wants to keep them overnight though to make sure they don't have any serious injuries. A couple of officers are on the premises to bring them in when they're released."

Jessica grinned wryly. "I'm still waiting for my noodle to bake." She retorted. "Have they been questioned?"

"Oh yeah..."

"And?"

"Well, apparently they were attacked by an unknown assailant."

Jessica's eyebrows raised in skepticism. "An unknown assailant, meaning a lone individual?"

"That's what they all claim, the ones able to talk that is."

"You mean to tell me that one lone individual single-handedly beat the crap out of five armed and dangerous men? I'm finding that a bit hard to believe."

Suddenly another female officer arrived at Jessica's desk and hurriedly produced a sheet of paper while urgently inserting herself into the conversation.

"We've got your man Detective."

Jessica took the print-out, examining it with a concentrated stare. "Thomas Lesco," she read aloud. "Assault with a deadly weapon charge. He looks like our guy the sketch artist rendered last night. Do we have a warrant for his arrest, Rachael?"

The blonde haired woman in police uniform smiled. "Ready and waiting."

Jessica quickly rose to her feet, saying not another word as she hurried from her desk, with Walter and Rachael quickly following her lead.

Chapter 5

The unmarked Crown Victorian squad car slowly eased to a stop at the side of the street, its headlights neutralized to keep Jessica's arrival as stealthy as possible. Walter and Rachael arrived in a like manner, their squad car parking behind her as she pulled a notepad from the inside pocket of her denim jacket. Carefully she scanned the address that was written on the paper, making sure that the place she had arrived at was the correct one.

Frowning, she shifted her gaze toward the house. Without taking her eyes off of the building, she vacated her vehicle, closing the door behind her as quietly as possible.

Looks like this is the place...

Silently, she scanned the house and its surrounding property as Walter and Rachael arrived at her side. The windows of the single story home seemed to stare almost ominously at her and her companions. Much of the house's white paint seemed to have eroded by time's passage, the large patches of exposed weather beaten wood marring the structure's appearance as it stood in eerie silence. Lying before the house's front porch was a barren flower bed, its lack of life and color serving as further evidence that very little care had been taken to maintain the place for quite some time.

"Not a single light on..." Walter stated while trying to see through the house's windows, the absence of light inside creating a sense of foreboding while hiding all from his sight.

"You think he's in there?" Rachael inquired.

Jessica frowned at the thought of possibly walking into a trap as she continued searching for evidence of Thomas Lesco's presence, knowing full well that he could be hiding in the darkness, waiting for their arrival. "Only one way to find out..."

Cautiously the trio began their approach, each keeping an ever watchful eye out for an ambush while making their way around the front of Jessica's car. Suddenly, Jessica's eyes caught the sight of movement behind one of the front windows, knowing it could only be one thing as the sound of shattering glass ended the surrounding silence.

"Gun!"

The blast from Thomas Lesco's weapon shook the night. Rachel released an ear-splitting scream as the bullet tore through her left shoulder, the impact twisting her torso as she crashed to the pavement.

"Shit!" Walter screamed as he and Jessica quickly took cover, a second shot striking the car's hood as Rachel desperately crawled to seek cover behind it as well. Jessica began to examine Rachel's wound as Walter used the car's radio to call for backup.

"Rachel..."

"I'll be okay..." she interrupted through clenched teeth. Blood poured from the wound, quickly staining her hand and uniform crimson as she clutched her shoulder.

"Just hold on Rachel..." Jessica drew her pistol and peeked over the hood of the car in an attempt to check on their attacker's position, ducking quickly back down again seconds before another shot hit the car.

"Thomas Lesco, you are under arrest!" She called out with authority. "Put down your weapon and come out with your hands above your head."

"Fuck you bitch!" Lesco shouted violently from within the darkened house. Two more bullets came for Jessica and her companions, making them hesitant to emerge from the protection that Jessica's car provided.

Quickly rising up from behind her cover, Jessica returned fire with a trio of shots. Thomas quickly darted behind the house's walls in avoidance, Jessica ducking down once more as well to avoid any return fire.

"We have to take him now." Jessica said, turning to Walter. "Cover me."

"Shouldn't we wait for backup?" Walter inquired. Two more bullets struck the car.

"Rachel needs help." Jessica protested. Walter cast a glance at Rachael. She barely clung to consciousness.

"We can't wait! We gotta get Lesco now!"

With reluctance etched in his face, Walter quickly rose from behind their cover, unleashing a barrage of shots at Thomas' hiding place. Round after round from Walter's pistol tore through the dark house as Jessica sprung from around the rear of her car. She swiftly made her way across the yard and to the back of the house as Walter to cover again.

From her new position, she could hear yet another gunshot from within the house. Hoping for the best, she slowly made her way toward its back door, her pistol aimed at the ground in a suppressed position as she crept along. Cautiously she opened the screen door, being wary of any creeks or groans that might alert Thomas of her entry.

Light was scarce in the kitchen that she had entered. The silhouettes of appliances, cabinets, and furniture where draped in darkness as only the faintest amount of light from the streetlights outside entered the room through a dirty window at her right. As quickly, yet quietly as possible, she negotiated an oval shaped wooden table and matching chairs that were in the room's center. The soles of her shoes touched softly upon the dirty tile flooring with each step taken as she advanced toward a doorway on the kitchen's opposite side.

Pressing herself against the edge of the doorway to conceal herself as best she could, she readied her pistol while peering into the next room. As with the kitchen, most of the living room was shrouded in the shadows, the area being mostly barren as a badly stained white carpet covered the floor. A worn recliner with a small pedestal style table sitting next to it, and a small television set atop a cheaply made cabinet were the only items in the room, their forms made visible by only the pale radiance that poured in from the streetlights outside.

Across the room, crouching beneath a shattered window, was the silhouette of Thomas Lesco. From the doorway she watched him, his back to her as he hastily set about the task of placing six more bullets into the cylinder of a revolver, seemingly unaware of her presence. Quickly she stepped into the room and turned her pistol on him.

"Freeze Lesco!"

Thomas remained motionless, his eyes widening in surprise at the sound of her voice.

"You are under arrest. Drop your weapon and place your hands in the air above your head."

Slowly, Thomas stood while extending his right hand out to his side, making his weapon easily visible. With a flick of his wrist, he tossed the gun aside; its landing upon the floor creating a dull thud as he slowly began to raise his hands.

"Keep your hands where I can see them." Jessica carefully began to advance. Keeping her gun at the ready, she began to extract her handcuffs.

Suddenly, Thomas spun around, ducking quickly as he lunged for the small end table nearby. With an upward scooping motion of his arm, he sent the table through the air at Jessica. Caught by surprise, she threw her arms up in a desperate defense against the sudden attack. Unable to fully block the assault, she staggered as the clawed foot of the table struck the side of her head.

Momentarily dazed, she was quickly seized by Thomas, her pistol easily wrested from her grasp as the front door suddenly burst open.

"Drop it Lesco!" Walter ordered as he entered the room, gun ready.

Thinking quickly, Thomas spun around to face the new threat, pulling Jessica in front of him while simultaneously pressing the barrel of her own gun to her temple.

Jessica gasped. Desperately she clutched at Thomas' left arm as it wrapped firmly around her neck.

"Drop the gun or I'll blow her fuckin brains out!"

"You don't wanna do this Thomas..." Walter suggested while maintaining his position. "Just let her go..."

Thomas tightened his grip. Jessica winced as he pressed the gun into her temple a little harder. "I SAID DROP THE FUCKIN GUN!"

Seconds later, Walter reluctantly began to lower his weapon.

"You're only making this worse for yourself." he warned in an attempt at reason.

"Toss the gun over here..."

"Don't do it..." Jessica warned with imploring eyes. "...he'll kill us both..."

Jessica shut her eyes tightly at the sound of Walter's gun hitting the floor. Desperately she fought to restrain her fear as police sirens could be heard in the distance. Walter put his hands up in surrender.

"Just let her go Thomas..." he said out of desperation." Just let her go and you can get out through the back door... I won't follow you... "

Thomas smiled malevolently. "You don't say..." he replied, "The back door huh... That's a good idea. You're pretty smart."

Cautiously, he began backing up, his hold on Jessica remaining as his intent to escape with her as his hostage became very clear.

"I'm not sure I trust you to stay here and not follow me though."

"Let her go Thomas."

"No dice man. Sorry, but I think I'll keep my hostage." Walter's eyes widened in horror as he stood powerless to stop Thomas' escape. "And you. You can just kiss your fat ass goodbye!"

With that, Thomas quickly removed the gun from Jessica's temple, a wild look in his eyes as he turned the weapon on Walter.

No longer held at gunpoint, Jessica seized her opportunity to strike. Quickly shooting her right hand downward, she seized Thomas by the groin, digging the tips of her fingers into the tender area with a claw-like grip. A high pitched scream erupted from him, his hold on her relinquished as his face twisted in agony. The pistol went off in his hand, the misfired shot harmlessly hitting the ceiling above as Walter dove to the floor.

Wasting no time in pressing her attack, Jessica released her grip, extending her arm straight out in front of her before bringing it back to strike

Thomas' face, the back of her elbow connecting with a sick crunch. Blood exploded from Thomas' nose, the force of the blow causing him to stagger as Jessica quickly turned to face him. Maintaining a sideways position, she crossed her legs to advance. With her left leg serving as a vertical base, she thrust her right leg out from her side, a scream of rage erupting from her as she delivered a powerful sidekick.

The heel of her foot slammed hard into Thomas' sternum. Launched off his feet, the gun flew from his grasp to land several feet away as he crashed to the floor.

"Jesus..." Walter said to himself in awe as Thomas lay at Jessica's feet, barely conscious.

Extracting her handcuffs, Jessica knelt beside him, proceeding to roll him onto his stomach as the increased volume of the wailing sirens heralded the arrival of police backup. Swirling flashes of red and blue light filled the darkened room. Jessica firmly cuffed Thomas Lesco's hands behind him while reading him his Miranda rights.

忍

Steam erupted from the black ceramic mug as Jessica filled it with coffee before replacing the pot into the maker's housing. Still somewhat shaken from the incidents surrounding Lesco's arrest, she sipped at the hot beverage in an attempt to further calm her edgy nerves. Out of her eye's corner, she spotted Rodger approaching.

"Hey." he said, a look of concern in his eyes as he filled his own cup. "I heard about what happened. You ok?"

Jessica managed a weak smile. "Well, despite my hostage experience I think I'll be alright." she replied before changing the subject.

"I thought you worked days?"

"I'm pulling a double shift." Rodger grinned.

Jessica reclaimed her file folder from beside the coffee maker. From amid the activities of the other police officers, she suddenly spotted the approach of the man she knew to be the police chief. Clad in a grey off the rack suit with a cornflower blue tie, his tall form bared a mien of authority as he strode nearer, signs of his near fifty years of age showing in the form of facial lines and graying hair. Stopping before her, he gazed at her with stern hazel eyes.

"Detective Devins..." he said with a nod.

"Chief Higgins..."

A brief moment of silence passed before he spoke again.

"Officer Benning, would you give me a moment with Detective Devins please?" he said, disguising his order in the form of a request.

"Yes sir." Rodger replied before hurrying off to other business.

A sigh escaped the chief before he would continue.

"How are you holding up?"

"I'll be ok." Jessica replied before trying to shift his attention to something other than her own wellbeing. "How's Rachel?"

"Officer Briggs is at the hospital with her now. From what I've been told she'll be out of action for a while, but she'll be fine."

Jessica smiled weakly as she sighed in relief.

"I don't really want to get into this now." Chief Higgins continued. "Lord knows you need time, but I'd really like to know what you thought you were doing when you attempted to apprehend Lesco alone tonight."

"I was thinking of Rachel's well-being." Jessica stated firmly. "I was thinking of every life that this

'Medicine Man' has ruined with the poisons that
he..."

"We all want the Medicine Man brought in
Jessica." The chief interrupted. "You're not alone in
this. Don't ever do something this foolish again."

Chief Higgins turned his attention from her.
Claiming a Styrofoam cup from the stack near the
coffee pot, he began filling it with coffee as he
continued.

"I want you out of here now. Come back when
you have had time to calm down. Tomorrow is
yours if you need it."

"Yes sir."

With that, Jessica proceeded to her desk.
Gathering her things, she made her way out of the
police station and to her car. Driving off, she was
unaware of the shadowy figure that silently
watched her from a rooftop across the street.

The opening and closing of the front door ended
the stillness about the house as Jessica entered.
Flicking a switch on the wall to light the room, she
hung her jacket to rest on a nearby coat rack before
making her way into the living room. Casually
discarding her police equipment onto the coffee
table, she seated herself on the sofa, removing her
shoes to leave them on the floor as she leaned back
to relax.

After several moments of quiet, she slowly turned
her head, her attention coming to rest on a small,
silver picture frame that sat upon the end table.
With her left hand, she took the photo from its spot
by her phone. A sigh escaped her as she gazed at
the photo of her and the man that was her father.

Jessica remembered well the day the photograph
had been taken; the day of her graduation from the

police academy. Side by side, before a wall of industrial gray stone they stood, both clad in the uniforms of Elmira's police officers. The gentle blue eyes of her father showed his love for family and life as he stood with his arm around her, clearly proud of his daughter's accomplishments as both presented a warm smile to whoever would gaze at the photograph.

Invading thoughts back to the time her father's demise began to replace the fonder memories of her achievements. Tears soon began to stream down her face in pale glistening lines as her anguish was rekindled.

I miss you so much...

Overcome with grief, she placed the picture face down on the coffee table. Slumping into a near fetal position on the sofa, she buried her face in her arms, her sobs continuing until she finally fell asleep.

Chapter 6

The window frame made not a sound as it slid upward, slowly pushed open by a hand clad in black. A gentle breeze sent its soft blue drapes to flow slightly as a masked visage cautiously peered inside. Weary of the fully lighted room, the dark figure slowly climbed through the open window, his soft, split toed boots touching silently onto the tan carpeted floor. Certain that no one from outside would see his entry at this late hour, he quickly scanned the room to be sure his entrance had gone undetected by the resident of the dwelling.

Light that emanated from an overhead fixture in the center of the living room's ceiling made all in the area clearly visible. Framed photographs of what he guessed to be the friends and family of the one living here adorned the white walls as he carefully looked about the room for what he sought. While making a mental note of the room's exits, his careful gaze passed over a cluttered computer desk at his left.

With caution he continued to negotiate the room, his weight carried on flexed knees as his search pressed on. Fluid and seamless were his movements, his body turning with catlike steps to scan the area. Moving past a fairly impressive entertainment center, he halted suddenly as his eyes came to rest on a coffee table and sofa that sat across the way. A pistol, a pair of handcuffs, a badge, a manila file folder, and a small picture frame that lay face down littered the table's surface. His eyes narrowed on the file folder, his movements to closer examine its contents ever cautious so as to not awaken the woman who slept on the sofa before him, the woman he knew to be Detective Jessica Devins.

Her legs curled up to accommodate the seats length as her chest slowly rose and fell, her breathing steady and relaxed as she peacefully slept. Still dressed in the jeans and t-shirt that he had seen her in earlier at the police station, it was apparent that her falling asleep in this spot had been quite unintentional. Beneath his mask, his eyes furrowed slightly as he noticed wet streaks leading away from her closed eyes.

She cried herself to sleep, but why?

Returning his attention to the coffee table before him, he claimed the small, silver plated picture frame, turning it face up to view the photo it held inside. He easily recognized the younger Jessica standing in police uniform, but the older man in the same uniform by her side was unfamiliar to him. Continuing to scan the photograph, he began to reach a conclusion as he noticed that she bore similarities to the tall dark haired man, particularly in the soft blue eyes that they both had.

Her father?

Deciding the matter to be something better looked into at another time; he replaced the picture, mindfully laying it face down as he had originally found it. Resuming his search, he picked up the manila file folder, certain that the information he needed would be found inside. He slowly flipped through the folder's contents. The papers inside were stamped in red with the word COPY as he thumbed quietly through them. His eyebrows sloped into a furrow as he suddenly came to a photograph of the man who had escaped him on this night as well as at Sutherton Park on the previous one.

Thomas Lesco, so that's his name...

Suddenly, he felt something gently brush against the ankle of his right leg. Turning his attention toward whatever the source could be, he spotted an orange tabby cat rubbing against him. The feline seemed to be well taken care of, with low purring sounds emanating from it as it affectionately brushed against his leg several times before curling up beneath the coffee table to go to sleep.

Nice kitty...

Returning to the task at hand, he continued to scan the next pages, mentally processing the information for tasks ahead. Closing the folder, he gently laid it back on the smooth surface of the table. Slowly, he turned to leave; his soft steps carrying him silently back to the open window through which he had earlier come through.

Pausing, he turned to cast one more glance over his shoulder at Jessica in her still undisturbed slumber. His eyes softened as he again pondered the source of her sorrow before resuming his exit. With the same stealthy precision that had gained him entry, he proceeded back out into the night, the window's drapes settling to stillness once more as it was silently slid shut.

Chapter 7

Jessica's eyes slowly opened, the rays of the sun pouring in through her living room's windows. Squinting, she pushed herself up to a seated position on the sofa, allowing her feet to come to rest upon the floor in an attempt to get the stiff feeling out of her cramped legs. With the back of her hands she rubbed her sleep filled eyes.

Slowly extending her arm, she claimed the cordless phone from its base to check the time. "Shit..." she groaned, seeing the time to be nine thirty AM. While silently chastising herself for last night's weakness as much as for oversleeping, she slowly stood to begin her day.

忍

"Glad they still serve breakfast around here..."

With a glazed doughnut in her left hand and a steaming cup of coffee in her right, Jessica stopped before her desk. Setting her goods down, she removed her denim jacket, sloppily draping it over the back of her chair before seating herself.

Scanning over the various paperwork that had arrived in her absence, she set about the task of sorting it while taking an occasional bite or drink.

A familiar voice snagged her attention from her work.

"How are you feeling Detective?"

Looking up, Jessica's eyes met those of Police Chief Higgins as he stood before her. "I'm hanging in there..." she replied with a weak smile and tired eyes.

"Are you sure you are up to this today?"

"I just don't wanna get behind on paperwork..."

Chief Higgins nodded stoically. "You are a very good cop Jessica, one of our best. We would hate to lose you because of reckless behavior."

She sat in silence, listening as the chief continued.

"I understand from firsthand experience where you're coming from. When you're out there on the streets and the pressure is on, sometimes life or death decisions have to be made. I just want you to be more careful out there in the future and to remember that finding this 'Medicine Man' is not your burden alone."

"I understand sir." She replied with a light smile. "I'll be out of here after I'm finished with this."

Chief Higgins grinned. "Very well, enjoy your day off Detective." With that, the chief took his leave.

"Thank you Sir, you have a good day too."

She set about continuing her paperwork, signing her name to documents that required a signature while eating on the go. With but a fraction of the mound of documents to complete, she stood with her coffee cup, intent on refilling it. As she briskly made her way around the front of her desk, her attention was suddenly snagged by something out of the ordinary.

Entering the police station was a newcomer. From the right hand of the tall, lean man hung a black leather Gucci briefcase. His suit looked expensive and well-tailored in a shade of deep navy blue, with an accompanying red silk tie that was vibrant against a white dress shirt. A fine, black leather trench-coat and matching gloves completed his impressive wardrobe, presumably to shield him from the slight chill of the air outside. From behind a pair of wire-rimmed spectacles, his eyes surveyed the area as he moved about with a stride of pure confidence.

Jessica watched as the dark-haired, immaculately groomed individual stopped to speak with one of her fellow officers, a handshake exchanged before the two would make their way across the precinct together. The man was escorted and introduced to Chief Higgins, a second handshake exchanged and a business card given before he and the newcomer would enter the Chief's office, disappearing behind a closed door.

Pondering what had just transpired, Jessica moved on to get her second cup of coffee.

"What was that about?" She asked a nearby officer while filling her mug.

"That was some hot-shot lawyer, from what I overheard." the officer replied while glancing back at the closed office door. "He was talking to the Chief about Thomas Lesco."

Jessica raised an eyebrow.

"You mean *that* is the lawyer we will be providing for Lesco?" She said with obvious disdain.

"Looks like it." the officer replied. "I would think the evidence against Lesco is overwhelming though. The bullets found at Sutherton Park traced back to the gun you found last night, which also had his prints all over it and was apparently obtained illegally. Lesco said he wasn't saying a word until he talked to an attorney. I guess that's his man. Seems like a nice guy though, really polite and all."

"Until he gets Thomas Lesco of the hook somehow..." Jessica added with an expression that looked as though she smelled something unpleasant.

Her eyebrows continuing to furrow, Jessica started back over to her desk. As she made her way, Chief Higgins and the attorney emerged from the office, their words more audible to her as she moved past them.

"Officer Mitchel, please escort Mr. Pierce to speak with Thomas Lesco." Chief Higgins instructed.

Pausing, Jessica cast a glance over her shoulder as Mr. Pierce and his escort began making their way to the cell blocks downstairs. As the attorney turned to leave, his gentle brown eyes met those of hers but for a fleeting moment, his gaze holding her briefly from behind his glasses. Turning away, Jessica continued her way back to her desk, wondering to herself if it was her imagination, or if the attorney's mouth actually shaped into a warm smile.

忍

All was silent in the cell of Thomas Lesco. Seated upon the cot in his confines, his hands lay clasped in his lap. A strip of medical tape crossed the bridge of his swollen, broken nose; the end result of a failed attempt to take Detective Jessica Devins as his hostage the previous night. With his head hung, he sullenly regarded the concrete floor between his feet as peach colored walls surrounded him.

Suddenly, he jerked up in alarm to the sound of a slamming door. Approaching footsteps followed, echoing about the walls of the cell block's corridor. Stopping before his cell was one of Elmira's finest. Beside the officer was a man clad in a suit and tie, an expensive looking briefcase in hand. Thomas quickly rose to his feet at the arrival of the newcomers.

"Your lawyer is here Lesco." The officer said before taking his leave. Thomas approached the bars of his cell as the attorney spoke.

"Greetings Mr. Lesco. I'm Jim Pierce, attorney at law." He said while making a slight adjustment to the glasses that he wore. "I will be representing your defense in court."

The attorney sat his briefcase upright on the floor beside him. Producing a business card from his suit's jacket pocket, he courteously offered it with a steady right hand. Thomas reached through the bars to claim the card.

"Never heard of you..."

Without warning, the attorney seized Thomas at the wrist of his outstretched hand. Quickly pulling him forward while pivoting slightly to his left, he shot his left hand through the bars, entangling his gloved fingers in a handful of Thomas' long ragged hair. With lightning speed, a simple ink pen was drawn from his jacket pocket, the point pressed firmly to Thomas' throat before a surprised gasp could escape him.

All was still again as Lesco's eyes widened in horror. Several seconds passed in deafening silence, the activity apparently going unheard as no one came to investigate. Thomas trembled in fear as he stared into the cold eyes of his attacker.

"As your attorney in this matter, I must advise you to keep your voice down." The man threatened.

"Who the fuck are you?!" Thomas gasped. His voice showed barely restrained panic as his face was pressed firmly between the bars of the cell.

"You haven't been too keen on speaking with me the past couple of nights." the man replied. "That's fine though. I have your full attention now I'm sure. I won't be taking too much of your time, just a few questions I want answered."

Thomas' eyes remained wide. His lip trembled like a small child as he suddenly realized who he faced.

"You!"

"I want the Medicine Man, Thomas. Who is he? Where is he?"

"I... I don't know..."

Thomas gasped yet again as the man he now knew to be his attacker from previous nights jerked hard on his crop of greasy hair. Threateningly, he pushed the pen into his neck a little harder.

"That wasn't the answer I was looking for, Thomas. Try again."

"Please! For the love of God!"

The man glared.

"I've never seen him. I've never seen the Medicine Man."

"Never?"

"He... His dealings with us are handled by another, a front-man."

Fear shined bright in Thomas' eyes.

"Now we are getting somewhere." The man whispered to him, smirking slightly. "Who is this front-man?"

忍

"Enjoy the rest of your day off Detective..."

"Thanks..." Jessica replied to another officer that bid her farewell. Slipping her arms into the sleeves of her denim jacket, she hastily gathered her things from her desk before proceeding toward the police station exit. As she moved amid the comings and goings of her peers, her ears managed to catch a portion of another conversation.

"Hello, I'm Jim Pierce attorney at law. I'm here to represent Mr. Thomas Lesco..."

Jessica froze. Slowly she looked over her shoulder, her eyes widening as she turned to see a dark haired man in a simple gray business suit, a handshake being exchanged between he and a young police officer.

Oh shit!

忍

"I'm gonna ask you one more time. Who handles the Medicine Man's dealings for him?"

Thomas felt a spasm of fear. Something liquid and warm began to run down his leg as he realized ashamedly that he was wetting himself.

"Please, don't... he'll kill me if I talk..."

The man raised an eyebrow. "You're in police lock-up, Thomas..." He said. "Not everyone can get to you like I have done. I'm pretty sure you're safe in here."

"That's what Robert Kane thought too!"

"What?"

Thomas grew pale, the look in his eyes showing that he had accidentally revealed too much.

Robert Kane...

Seconds passed with the pause of thought, the man's facial expression slowly shifting to one of utter shock.

No...

A horrifying realization suddenly came to him. "Someone with the police is helping the Medicine Man?!" he asked, the shock of the revelation forcing the question out of him even in his certainty that such was the case.

Thomas only stared in silent fear as more questions desperately came.

"Robert Kane was murdered wasn't he? He was murdered by someone working with the police!"

Thomas uttered not another word. The silence spoke volumes.

Jessica rushed toward the stairway leading down to the cell blocks, other officers looking on to ponder her sudden haste as she dashed past them. Quickly she descended the stairs, taking the steps two at a time. Nearing the bottom of the stairway, she spotted the awaiting officer. Seated contently in a chair next to the sturdy door to the cell block entrance, he read a newspaper.

"Open the door!" She instructed urgently. Her breath hitched in her chest, as she reached the bottom of the steps.

"What's going on Detective?" The officer asked in confusion, looking up from his reading.

"Open the damn door!"

The officer hurriedly produced the keys as he stood, his newspaper falling to the floor in his haste. With the officer in tow, Jessica dashed through the opened doorway, her heart pounding as she tried to ready herself for whatever lay ahead.

Upon entering, Jessica's eyes widened in surprise. Down the corridor, barely fifteen feet away, was the attorney that had come to see Lesco. The fact that the lawyer wasn't what he seemed to be was now clear as he held Thomas roughly by the hair while pressing something threateningly to his throat, closer examination revealing his weapon to be a simple pen.

At the sound of Jessica and the other officer's hurried entry, the man quickly released his hold on Thomas, who quickly staggered backwards from the bars to escape his attacker. In a flash, the man's right foot struck out at his briefcase on the floor beside him. It sailed through the air at Jessica and the officer, both caught off-guard by the sudden flying object as they desperately raised their hands to block it.

Taking advantage of the sudden distraction, the man charged. With a hard shove, he sent Jessica and the other officer to the floor while dashing past, the officer being incapacitated as the back of his head bumped the concrete in the fall.

"Stop!" Jessica yelled as the man began racing up the stairs.

While regaining her footing, she tossed a quick glance at the fallen officer. Seeing him to be momentarily dazed but otherwise alright, she charged after the intruder. From the bottom of the stairs, she saw him produce a black hood of some sort from beneath his coat. Quickly, he slipped the hood over his head, covering his identity as he reached the stairway's apex.

"Stop that man!"

Jessica's warnings did not go unheard, several other police officers already on their way to investigate the commotion as the masked man emerged through the doorway. Seeing that he was now cut-off from the front doors through which he had originally entered, and would have to find an alternate exit, he quickly lunged for a nearby desk. Clearing it of most of its paperwork, he flung a mass of file folders at his pursuers, the scattering papers temporarily hindering their advance. Hearing quickly falling footsteps at his rear, he turned his head to spot Jessica as she emerged from the cell blocks below.

Jessica lunged, her hand shooting out and seizing hold of the man's tie as he leaped back, the tie coming off in her grasp to reveal it as a simple clip on. The man grabbed a nearby chair, tipping it to fall between him and Jessica as he turned towards the stairs to the next floor. With Jessica's pursuit briefly hindered, he made it to the stairs, his coat trailing behind him as the mob of officers continued their chase.

With at least a dozen policemen on his tail, the man grabbed the lapels of his coat. Quickly pulling it clear of his shoulders, he flung his arms straight out behind him, slipping them from its sleeves as it dropped into the face of the nearest pursuing officer. Losing his footing, the blinded officer stumbled backwards into his fellows, their chase again hindered as the man continued on. With a handful of other officers at her back, Jessica negotiated the fallen and flailing bodies on the stairs to make the ascent.

Reaching the next floor, the man was met by yet more law enforcement personnel, who had been alerted that something was wrong by the commotion on the floor below them. With the officers unprepared for his sudden appearance, the man swiftly secured a fire extinguisher from a nearby wall-mount. CO_2 filled the air in billowing clouds as he blasted his attackers with the canister's contents. Moving amid the blinded officers, he began making his way towards a fire escape at the room's opposite side.

Through the thick white haze, the man turned to spot Jessica as she charged into the room, ever persistent in her chase. From the room's center, he hurled the nearly spent fire extinguisher at her as she came forward. Thinking quickly, Jessica ducked, the canister sailing over her head to strike an officer who had the misfortune to be at her rear.

Closing with her masked foe, Jessica sprung forward with a hop off her right foot. Landing upon her left, her right leg lashed out with a quick snapping motion as she attempted to drive the ball of her foot into the man's abdomen. With lightning speed, the man executed a pivot like movement, hopping to the inside of her front kick as his leg moved back to effortlessly turn his body to a side profile, Jessica's foot striking only the empty space he had once occupied before returning to the floor.

Fighting on, she launched a quick jab with her right fist before bringing her left in with a cross, a furious cry erupting from her with each punch. Quickly the man ducked, avoiding the attempted jab at his face. Bringing his left leg to his rear while stepping back defensively, he allowed much of his weight to rest on his rear leg. Rocking back, he positioned his left hand to defend his face while swinging his right up in an outward sweeping motion. The knuckles of his fist struck the lower portion of Jessica's attacking arm, a cry of pain erupting from her as the extremity was blasted away by the unorthodox blow.

Rocking forward, the man lifted his rear leg. Flexing and folding it to raise the knee up to his shoulder, he kicked straight out with a downward lateral motion that much resembled an over exaggerated step. The heel of his foot slammed into Jessica's abdomen with bone jarring force, knocking her onto her back. Helplessly stunned and prone, she watched breathlessly as the man fled for the fire escape, other officers emerging from the floor below to charge after him. Slowly she struggled to stand, her breath coming in ragged gasps as she nursed her stomach.

Reaching the fire escape, the man leaped over the platform's railing, a gasp escaping from Jessica as gravity took him towards the pavement. With cat-like agility, he flexed his legs upon impact, his body lowering to the pavement to take away the shock of landing. Executing a forward roll over his right shoulder, he swiftly returned to his feet once more, dashing across the police precinct's parking lot to vanish in the city's mid-morning activity.

Jessica managed to get to her feet as several officers rushed past her, cries of "Go!" and "Hurry!" filling the air as they lowered the fire escape's ladder. Holding her arm, she trudged out to the platform and peered down at the lot below, with no sign of the masked man to be seen. Breathing heavily, she watched as the officers descended the ladder as quickly as possible.

A sense of awe filled her. Never before had she seen such determined athleticism and survivalist instinct. Below her, the officers scrambled about the precinct's parking lot, combing the area in what she knew to be a futile search. The man was gone.

So much for my day off...

Chapter 8

Jessica leaned her head back, her eyes closing as the hot bath water soothed her tired, aching body. A soft sigh escaped her as she slid a little deeper into the tub, the back of her head coming to rest gently on the tub's rim as her form submerged beneath soap and bubbles. Remaining like this for several moments she began to reflect on the events of the day.

Total bedlam had ensued in the police precinct following the escape of the masked infiltrator. With the mayor putting heat on the department after the incident, Chief Higgens ordered total media blackout regarding the disturbance. Linking the man to the Sutherton park incident with Thomas Lesco and the alley assault the previous night was done with little difficulty.

Despite the department's best efforts, the police could get little information from the Thomas Lesco. "It was a ninja! A real fuckin ninja!" He would repeatedly claim before being decidedly put under a stricter watch. Speculation ran rampant as to the cleverly disguised man's identity and motivations, with Chief Higgins gathering the department for a meeting.

"Those pushers that we picked up all claim it was one guy who attacked them." one officer stated.

"Yeah," another added. "All done up in a black suit and hood from what they described. Lesco swears up and down that it was a ninja."

There was a chorus of chuckles.

"I bet he's some rich guy." still another officer started with cheery sarcasm. "A millionaire by day and crime fighting vigilante by night."

Howls of laughter filled the room from the other officers. Chief Higgins was not amused. "I think you've been watching too much T.V." Jessica said in a good natured tone.

"I don't care what TV shows you all watch." Chief Higgins said sternly. The scowl on his face banished the lighthearted mood as all grew silent. "I'm glad you're all having fun here because this damn guy just made a laughing stock of our whole department. No one takes the law into their own hands in this city. I want this nutcase found, and taken off the streets."

With that, and Higgins dismissal, the other officers would take their leave.

Soon after an APB was put out for anyone fitting the intruder's vague description, Jessica went home as initially intended, anxiously awaiting news of any new findings by the department. With her time off, she would take care of other endeavors, chores that she had been shirking exponentially. Being an adept house keeper but not an efficient one, her home tended to clutter. Stacks of unread magazines and newspapers had begun to litter the floor beneath her coffee table. Clean, unfolded clothes remained in a basket by her bedroom door. The fridge was bare except for a half gallon of milk and several bottles of condiments. Thus, her free time was spent grocery shopping, tidying her house, sorting her mail, and folding her clothes, all in all a rather anticlimactic day compared with the morning's events.

Jessica's thoughts gradually returned to the current moment as her bath water was beginning to cool. Bringing her bath to a conclusion, she dried herself in a large soft towel and slipped into a pink cotton night gown. Making her way to her kitchen, she set about fixing herself a glass of ice tea. Suddenly, a familiar mewing grabbed her attention as soft fur brushed against her calf. She looked down to see her cat sitting up on its haunches, the feline looking up with imploring eyes as it meowed a second time, drawing out the cry pitifully for attention.

"I hear you Buster..." she cooed to the cat with a wry grin. "You're hungry, huh?"

She indulged the cat with a saucer of milk that she poured from the counter, the cat immediately beginning to lap up the milk once it was placed upon the floor. She then prepared a microwave dinner to remedy her own hunger.

With food and drink in hand she made her way into the living room. Seating herself comfortably on the couch, she tucked her bare feet up next to her as she claimed the television controller, the TV coming to life with the press of a button.

Continuing to aim the remote with an extended right hand, she changed the channel several times before stopping on a local station, taking an interest in the news program that was in progress. While contently dinning on Salisbury steak, mashed potatoes, and a chocolate brownie, she watched as a weather man gave the forecast for warmer weather in the upcoming days.

A noise suddenly intruded on her peace as the telephone rang insistently beside her, calling her attention away from the TV. "Hello?" she answered.

"Detective Devins?"

"Yeah Walter it's me." She replied, at once recognizing the chipper voice on the other end. "What have you got for me?"

"Well, I hate to tell you this..." he began. His voice was sullen, as though to prepare her for bad news.

"But we've hit another dead end, right?" Jessica interjected.

"Afraid so Detective, I'm real sorry. The briefcase was full of dummy paper work, most where random printouts from newspaper articles. Just to look official, you know? The glasses were non-prescription and his coat and tie are available in several clothing stores just in town, probably hundreds across the state. They're nice, but fairly common. Probably purchased with cash, there's no way to trace the purchases."

"Damn." Jessica swore.

"This guy is all anyone around here can talk about tonight." Walter continued. "Night shift heard all about it from the day-time guys. I heard you pulled some *Dirty Harry* stuff and tried to take him."

"He's good, whoever he is." Jessica admitted. "I've tussled with guys before who had some martial arts experience, but nothing like that. The way this guy moved, and how he hit, his whole fighting style, it was unique. I've never seen anything like it before."

"Did he really come in dressed like a lawyer to get to Lesco?" Walter inquired.

"Yeah, he did. He was good enough to fool all of us and get down to the cells. He was even flashing around legitimate looking business cards and shaking everyone's hand. We got an APB on the guy, but something tells me we're wasting our time looking."

"Sounds like we got a hell of a vigilante Detective..."

"How is Rachael doing?" Jessica asked, changing the subject.

"She's gonna be alright. I'll probably stop by and see her again in a day or two."

"Give her my best, ok?"

"Will do Detective, you take care."

"You too, Walter. Bye, bye."

With her conversation with Walter concluded, Jessica hung up the phone. Continuing to dine, she watched in annoyance as commercials had now appeared in place of the news program that she was watching before. The ads drawled by as she scooped the last of the potatoes on to her fork. Suddenly the phone rang again.

"Well, aren't I popular tonight..." she said to herself with mock whimsy.

Casually she answered the phone again.

"Hello?"

"Is this Jessica Devins?" an unfamiliar male voice inquired pleasantly.

"Yes it is."

Her eyes narrowed as she hated sales calls and was wary of unknown callers.

"*Detective* Jessica Devins?" The man asked again, emphasis on her occupation as a law enforcement officer.

"Yes, this is she." She frowned while confirming her identity. A salesman would never use her job title. "Who is this?"

"Please forgive me for calling like this, Detective." The man said apologetically. "I hope I'm not interrupting anything. We had a chance encounter earlier today it seems, at the station."

A look of shock formed on Jessica's face as she sat up rigid on the couch. Several seconds passed as she remained silent, unable to form words as the startling realization of who was on the phone began setting in.

"Are you still there Detective?"

Jessica swallowed, forcing down a lump in her throat. "Yes." she finally said unsteadily. Her stomach squirmed in nervous knots like uncoiling snakes. This man knew her home phone number. He more than likely knew her address as well. Unsure of this man's motives, she began to ponder her safety.

"I would like to offer my apologies for our previous meeting." he continued.

"Apologies?" Jessica repeated in surprise, deciding it was best to let him do most of the talking. She glanced about the room, her mind wandering to the issue .40 pistol in her bedroom.

"Yes Detective, I truly hope that none of the other officers or yourself where seriously hurt in our regrettable conflict earlier. Your department left me little choice but to defend myself."

Jessica remained unsure of how to handle the situation. The man's voice didn't seem at all what she would have expected from the one who wielded the combat skills that bested her and her fellow officers. His voice held, strangely enough, gentleness in it.

"Well..." Jessica finally started, deciding to go with the flow of the conversation for the moment, hoping that casual talk would aid her in learning more about the man. "I don't think anyone was seriously injured, they seemed alright when I left."

"I'm glad to hear that." The man responded, sounding surprisingly relieved.

Jessica's face twisted into a look of confusion, the muscle between her eyes pinched with a questioning look as she was unsure of what to say next.

"So... umm..." she began hesitantly. "People are saying you're a Ninja. Is that true? I mean, are you seriously a Ninja?" She wanted to smack her head with her free palm. The question had sounded rather flat and lame. A slight twinge of embarrassment shot through her.

God that was stupid...

"I am a practitioner of their martial ways, yes." he replied, sincerity clear in every word. "You seem to be a martial artist yourself."

"I practice Wing Chun." She stated, wondering immediately afterward if she had revealed too much of herself to this man. She decided more caution was in order while speaking to him.

"Ahh..." He proclaimed with recognition. "A style of Chinese Kung Fu... very impressive..."

"You're familiar with it?" Jessica said, the question sounding as much like a statement. Her face showed a hint of surprise, as the man's knowledge of the martial arts in general seemed quite extensive. "Also called Wing Chun Kuen," he continued, "It gets its name from a woman named Yim Wing Chun who was taught by a Buddhist nun. Translates roughly into 'Beautiful Spring-time Fist or such I believe?"

"Yeah..." Jessica said in an astonished tone. "Yeah that's right."

"Did you know that Japan's first Ninja where men who emigrated from China?"

"I didn't know that." She replied with a tone of interest, hoping to veil her attempts at learning more about the man through their common interest in martial arts. "I'm not very familiar with your style; I didn't know anyone really practiced anything like that."

"It's a very antiquated method." He said.

"I see... So how does one become a Ninja then? Is it like it is in the movies?"

"Hollywood hardly portrays the Ninja correctly." He replied, a twinge of amusement in his tender voice. "One doesn't have to travel to some far off mountain top in the wilds of Japan to locate a wise old man in a Pagoda, nor are we the assassins cloaked in black that you would see in any cheap martial art film. But I think you're more interested in finding out who I am, rather than in talking shop with me. Would I be correct in that assumption Detective?"

Jessica shuddered. She could sense a sudden barrier coming between them, their conversation seeming more adversarial.

So much for a subtle approach...

A sigh escaped her as she laid her head back against the couch. "What you're doing is against the law." she said with a twinge of exasperation.

"A regrettable, yet necessary course of action, I assure you Detective." The man replied. "If there were other avenues to take, believe me, I would do so."

Jessica remained silent as he continued.

"It is unfortunate that circumstances have placed you in a position of opposition to me. I simply want the same thing you do."

"And what is that?"

"Justice, Detective. I shall keep you on the phone no longer, as I have things I must attend to. I must give you a warning though, before I leave."

"A warning?"

Jessica's eyebrows furrowed, her lips forming a thin tight line. She imagined the words to come, her heart thumping in equal parts fear and anger. Her hands began to tremble.

"Oh, a warning, huh?" She said, unable to keep the edge from her voice as her ire began to rise. "Stay out of your way, I guess? Or you'll kill me, right? I don't take kindly to threats, who-ever the hell you are."

"I find your preconceived notions of me to be appalling Detective." The man said calmly. "And to be honest, a little hurtful."

Jessica's face took a look of puzzlement.
Hurtful?
Her eyes softened, her whole body slumping backwards against the couch. "I... I didn't mean to..."

"Forget about it Detective." the man interrupted, "It's not important."

"What is it that you needed to warn me about?" She finally asked.

"Someone in your Department is working for the Medicine Man."

"What?"

Jessica sat up again. Her mind raced. She could think of nothing the man could gain from such a fabrication. He had to be telling the truth.

"Who?" she finally asked.

"I wish I knew Detective. Your untimely arrival unfortunately hindered my attempts to gather any more information."

"Lesco told you this?"

"In so many words, I believe he knows who this individual is."

"I appreciate you telling me this," Jessica said. "As an officer of the law though, I must insist that you stop what you're doing."

"I'm afraid I can't do that Detective."

"What you're doing is vigilantism." Jessica warned reasonably. "I can't abide this, nor can my department."

Please tread carefully, Detective. You could be in more danger then you realize. I wouldn't want you to suffer a fate similar to your..."

Jessica's breath caught in her chest with a hitch, her eyes again widening in surprise. She knew full well what the man was about to say.

"You... you know about my father?"

"Please forgive me. I shouldn't have brought it up."

"How did you…" She was unable to finish her inquiry.

"I am not without resources of my own Detective."

Jessica remained silent, not trusting her voice to stay steady. Her eyes stung slightly, causing her to blink rapidly as she tried not to succumb to her personal anguish again.

"Believe me; I know what it is like to lose someone close… someone you care about." The man said softly after a bout of silence. "You truly have my sympathy Jessica."

Her eyes began to water. Oddly enough, the man calling her by name triggered the tear. He began to feel more personal now, like a close friend rather than a stranger over the phone. "You know about my pain, why not share yours?" Jessica uttered tremulously, still attempting to learn more about this man.

"Under different circumstances, I would like nothing more." He replied. "I believe its best you know as little about me as possible though."

"Yeah." Jessica said somberly, her voice thickening as unshed tears stung her eyes. "It probably is…" She found a part of herself wishing that she could share with this man, as they seemed to have more in common than she could have realized, the possible motivations for his actions becoming apparent.

"I must go now… Please take care…"

"Wait…"

It was too late. The man had hung up. Jessica held the receiver in her hand, the repetitive beeping that soon followed the line's disconnection blaring harshly in her ear. A sigh of frustration escaped her as she angrily hung up. Standing, she made her way across the living room to her window. Wiping her eyes, she stared out into the night, silently reaching a conclusion.

It's time I learn the secrets of the Ninja...

Chapter 9

Ninja. The word seemed almost absurd to Jessica as she typed it into an online search engine. The activities of other police officers continued around her. While waiting for the search results, she briefly looked up from her monitor. Watching the other officers on the move, she remembered the ninja's warning from last night.

She frowned at the thought of a co-worker helping the Medicine Man, working unseen to hinder her department's efforts while he flooded Elmira's streets with drugs and crime from behind a veil of secrecy. Silently, she pondered which of those possessing a badge hid the taint of corruption.

It could be anyone...

Forcing herself to put those thoughts aside, she returned her gaze to the computer screen, the results of her search now displayed. Her face lengthened in surprise, her eyebrows rising as she seen the number of websites her search produced, so many dedicated to ninjas. Everything from movies to toys to motorcycles, the number of results being well into forty thousand.

Jesus...

Sighing, she slowly began scrolling through the list with the computer's mouse.

After several seconds of scrolling past unlikely pages, a title in bold letters suddenly grabbed her attention.

The Ninja Demystified She clicked on the title, the webpage opening after a few moments of loading. *As good a place as any to start looking...*

The Ninja Demystified

Hello and welcome to my little corner of the internet. This website is dedicated to... That's right, Ninjas. Why? Because I think they are cool! :D

Many hours of diligent research went into the creation of this website and I hope, as a fellow Ninja enthusiast, that you enjoy it :)

Jessica clicked on the 'print' icon on her screens toolbar. Clicking and whirring sounds emanated from the ancient printer as it came to life, the device being the best department funds could currently supply. After a few moments, it ejected three pages, the front of all bearing the web-pages contents. After claiming the printouts, Jessica gathered her other belongings and set out for a quiet place to continue her research.

The soft chirping of birds called out all around, a sense of serenity filling the mild spring air as it often does when outside in warm, pleasant weather. Jessica sat at a park picnic table, its top

tagged with graffiti by teen loiterers. A cool breeze caressed her bare arms even as the bright sun warmed the top of her head, her hair warm against her neck. Surrounded by trees and abandoned playground equipment, she enjoyed the quiet atmosphere as school still hadn't been let out for the day. Sipping every so often from a can of soda, she settled in to read the rest of the print outs for her research.

Origins and History of the Ninja

Although the ninja have been portrayed as spies and assassins through various entertainment mediums, there is in truth, little evidence to support such claims in historical accounts. Tracing the history and origins of the Ninja is difficult at best. According to many sources however, their origins can be linked to immigrants who had fled from China after the fall of the T'ang Dynasty in 907.

Jesus...

Jessica's thoughts returned to the man who had called her last night, and his mention of the first to become ninja.

These men found refuge in Japan's mountains, where their religious practices, mind and body fortification skills, and their understanding of nature were accepted by samurai that were willing to follow a different path; one with a different understanding of man, nature, and combat relation.

This concept took root in many small villages of Japan's Iga and Koga regions during the 11th and 12th centuries. Later, the 15th and 16th centuries would see the ninja at the height of their power. Their feats during these times became legendary, and the shadowy warriors would be credited with mystical powers such as invisibility, teleportation, shape changing, and even the ability to read minds.

Out of fear of their success and military power, General Oda Nobunaga launched an extermination campaign in hopes of annihilating the ninja clans in 1581. Although finally successful in overwhelming the ninja families, their survivors spread through other regions to continue passing their art and knowledge to other generations.

In 1603, Ieyasu Tokugawa became shogun, and rather than try to eliminate the ninja, he would use them as his personal bodyguards. With the ninja's capacity to gather intelligence, the Tokugawa era would eventually bring unity and civil order to Japan. Ironically it would be peace that would bring about the end of the ninja, as their skills would no longer be needed in the tranquil times. Today, the last of Japan's true ninja families are believed to be gone.

Jessica shook her head in near disbelief at the extent of the ninja's history.

Unbelievable! This guy is for real!

The ninja appeared to be no more, and yet the man she sought seemed to wield the very skill and power that had made them into legends. Her interest deepening, she turned the page to read on.

Ninja Combat

Ninjutsu, which translates into the "art of invisibility," focuses on a wide array of combat tactics, as well as espionage skills and spiritual training. Known as the "Ninja Juhakkei," their training seemed to be comprised of 18 different disciplines. Although some were shared by the samurai as well, the techniques of each discipline were approached differently by the ninja.

Seishin Teki Kyoyo (Spiritual Refinement)

Taijutsu (Unarmed Combat)

Tantojutsu (Knife Fighting)

Kenjutsu (Swordsmanship)

Bojutsu (Stick Fighting Arts)

Shurikenjutsu (Throwing Blades)

Yari & Naginata (Spear Fighting)

Kusarigama & **Kyoketsu Shoge** (Chain & Sickle Weapons)

Kayakujutsu (Use of Fire & Explosives)

Hensojutsu (Disguise & Impersonation)

Shinobi Iri (Stealth Entering Methods)

Bajutsu (Horsemanship)

Sui Ren (Water Training)

Bo-ryaku (Strategy)

Cho Ho (Espionage)

Intonjutsu (Escape & Concealment Using the Elements)

Ten-mon (Meteorology)

Chi-mon (Geography)

The Nin

The Japanese character for Ninjutsu's 'Nin' translates into 'stealth' or 'secrecy' as well as 'endurance' or 'perseverance'. The character is actually comprised of two separate characters, the top one meaning 'blade', while the bottom character means 'heart', for a proper interpretation of "Although you hold a blade over my heart, I will endure."

Blade   **Heart**   **Nin**

Ninjutsu Today

While those interested in the Ninja's combat arts should be aware of dubious imposters who are interested only in separating one from his money, there are in actuality, instructors who do teach the authentic martial arts of the Ninja. Some stick to the traditional arts while others have modernized the style to better suit today's lifestyles. Below is a list of websites worth visiting for those interested in learning more about the Ninja or Ninjutsu.

Jessica scanned over the list of websites, deciding to check some of them from her private computer at home. Quickly finishing her beverage, she stood to leave. Folding her research material to accommodate storage in her jeans, she slid the papers into her hip pocket where they caused a slight indentation. In route to her vehicle, she discarded her empty soda can into a nearby trash receptacle that was positioned next to a tree in the park.

She briskly made her way around the front a silver 2000 Impala that was her personal car. As she began to enter her vehicle she noticed a new sound reaching her ears, drowning out the pleasant singing of the birds as its volume gradually increased. A sense of dread began to swell up inside her, her eyes widening as she recognized the roaring sound to be that of a fast approaching automobile.

At instinct's command, Jessica quickly dove away from her car. Out of her peripheral vision, she saw only a mass of blurred white, the volume of the engine's roar peaking in her ears as a vehicle plowed through the space she had occupied only a moment before. Catching herself with her hands as she landed chest first in the middle of the street, she quickly pushed herself up to one knee.

Instinctively she drew her side arm, her finger compressing the trigger a fraction as she took aim at the retreating vehicle. Almost at once, a dirty white Oldsmobile that she saw beyond her sights disappeared from view as it rounded a corner at break-neck speed, the sound of its screeching tires fading as the car sped out of sight.

With clenched teeth, Jessica shakily hurried to her feet. Holstering her firearm, she quickly ran to her car, where she radioed the police station to report the attempted hit and run. Breathing heavily, she silently stared off in the direction that the car had gone, her eyebrows furrowing as her heart pounded maddeningly in her aching chest.

Shit...

Chapter 10

J essica's mind wandered as she drove along. Pondering past events, she stared ahead. Two days had passed since the attempted hit and run, which had left her on edge when out in the open. Police were unsuccessful in locating the vehicle, nor was a suspect able to be found, as anyone could have been hired to do it. There was no doubt in her mind that whoever it was among her colleagues that secretly aided the Medicine Man was hindering her attempts to get new leads in the investigation.

Without a clue as to who the corrupt officer might be, or indeed any proof of police corruption, she didn't dare show her suspicions of foul play, especially with her only lead on the matter being a masked man who was now himself pursued by the justice system. She knew only one who could give her the answers she needed.

Thomas Lesco...

An interrogation would have to be conducted with subtlety however. The fact that her suspicions where unknown to anyone on the force was her only advantage at this point. For now, she would continue playing ignorant, knowing that only through carefully planned action could she solve this case. She smirked slightly as she thought back to the Japanese character for ninjutsu's Nin, and how ironic it was that its meaning of stealth and secrecy, as well as endurance and perseverance had now become her proverbial bread and butter.

Like her quest to bring the Medicine Man to justice, her search for the elusive ninja was also proving difficult. She had checked all the websites and instructors she had found online, with most claiming to never teach the ninja's legendary stealth methods, as such arts could easily be used for ill intent. Those few who did teach the espionage skills of the Ninja were very cautious of who they chose to impart this knowledge on. Extensive background checks where in the norm, and the students had to prove themselves to be of noble character while remaining with their teachers for many years. Jessica's own background checks brought up no one that would have a motive to pursue the Medicine Man, thus leaving her to surmise that the one she sought had somehow acquired their skills in the distant lands where the ninja was born.

Slowing the Impala, she steered into a parking lot beside of her destination. Exiting her vehicle once parked, she instinctively checked both ends of the lot for anyone who seemed suspicious, a caution she had to maintain if someone was willing to stop her by any means. She hurried to the main entrance of the place that her research into the ninja would continue, the Elmira Public Library.

The gray stone building, with its high shaded windows, had an institutional look about it. One not being a resident of Elmira could easily pass the library and never know what it was, as its main entrance and big lettered sign were facing a side alley, as well as an elevated rail for trains. She walked around the corner of the building to its entrance, passing a bronze plaque on the wall that commemorated the building's history. Reaching the entrance, she pushed into the heavy shaded glass doors before walking into a small industrial carpeted foyer, where two benches of black pipe metal sat against the stone wall.

Continuing on, Jessica turned and pushed into the main entrance doors, their clear glass construction making them much lighter than the first. The library's interior was much more pleasant than its drab exterior. The color of the walls was a warm cream, the floor tiled in brown with spaces of darker brown carpeting beneath areas occupied by tables and cushioned chairs. The first floor was large, with a section devoted to the rental of educational DVDs. Several of the tables were occupied by high school students who worked on end of the year projects, as well as a few older people from the Elmira College. The center of the first floor seemed very spacious with an impressive set of spiral stairs extending to the second floor while wrapping about in a giant veranda. In the center of the veranda, a large Chinese parade dragon and several oriental kites of elaborate design hung from the ceiling, giving the place a wash of bright colors that drew the eye almost at once.

Jessica approached the handsome maple wood counters, where several computers hummed. A librarian sat on a roll-a-round chair, the young brown haired man appearing very tidy in khaki pants and a white dress shirt as he busily arranged cards that where needing to be filled.

"Excuse me..." Jessica said politely to get the man's attention. Looking up from his work, the man smiled pleasantly, his face long and pointed as he spoke with a friendly tone.

"Good afternoon ma'am. Can I help you with something?"

"Well," Jessica began. "I'm actually trying to research a martial art called 'Ninjutsu'. I was hoping you might be able to help me out."

The young man reflected silently as he turned to the computer, his keystrokes clicking sharply as he brought up the library's search forum. "Well, let's have a look see. If we don't have anything, the Corning Library might."

Jessica stood patiently, awaiting the librarian's search results.

忍

Jessica glanced briefly at the single book she was able to acquire, the only one on the subject of ninjutsu that the library had. Returning her gaze to the road ahead, she amusingly pondered the possibility of the ninja that she pursued checking out this very book for leisurely reading of his own. Pressing down on the accelerator, she sped up to go with the flow of the afternoon traffic.

Traveling on, she soon caught sight of the building she knew to be the Arnot Hospital. The white brick building and galvanized steel entrance was a pride to Elmira. State-of-the-art laboratories and surgical facilities where housed there along with some of the finest doctors and surgeons in New York state. Great white letters on a blue back drop proclaimed the name above its glass entrance doors.

As she came closer to the large parking lot in front of the building, she recognized a Crown Victorian of the Elmira police department, the number on the plate being easily familiar to her.

Walter...

Giving a quick turn signal, she veered into the parking lot, surmising Walter to be there paying Rachael a visit.

She needed help from someone, and knew that if she could trust anyone, she could trust Walter, as he had been on the force for years, and had been there to assist with Lesco's arrest. Quickly securing the first available parking space on the lot, she hurried towards the hospital, its automatic doors sliding open for her as she approached. She entered the slightly elevated waiting room and reception desk area, colorful paintings of flowers and wilderness scenes hanging from the white walls to greet her. Thick plush chairs on a blue carpet surrounded a television set that hung from the wall as she approached the semi-circular desk of the receptionist, a large vase of spring daisies catching her eye as they sat in the arcing desk's center, forming a divider between two women who sat at the computers.

Jessica approached a middle-aged, harassed looking woman in the whites of a hospital uniform, who looked up as she came forward.

"Hello, May I help you?"

Jessica smiled at the woman's friendly demeanor. "Yes, I'm here to see a friend of mine, Rachel Dawson."

The women clicked a few keys on her keyboard. "Oh yes, Miss Dawson is on the second floor in the B wing, her room number is 34D. Use the elevators right around the corner here and they'll take you up to her wing." She motioned to a hall off to her left instead of the elevators next to her on the right.

Jeeze, this place is huge.

"Thank you." Jessica replied with a smile before going down the hallway the women had indicated. Finding the elevators, she entered one and proceeded to the second floor. From there, obtained directions from a passing orderly enabled her to finally find what was referred to as the 'D Suite'.

Moving down the hall, she began checking the numbers until she found Rachel's room, its door slightly ajar as voices she recognized to be Walter's and Rachael's came from inside. As a gesture of courtesy, she rapped gently on the solid door frame with her middle knuckles before peeking inside.

"Hi..." she greeted with the quiet tone one usually adopts when in a hospital.

"Hi Jessica!" An excited Rachel said, seeming to be in good spirits while sitting up against the bed's headboard, propped upright with plush pillows. Seated next to the bed on a large cushioned chair, was Walter, who smiled while greeting Jessica a little wave.

"Hi Walter."

Jessica stepped into the room. "How are you feeling?" she asked, addressing Rachel in a more upbeat voice.

"Doing pretty good, they got me on pain medicine but I don't need it as much now. They said I can go home tomorrow. I won't be back to work for a while though, two to three weeks the doctor said." Jessica smiled, this being the first good news she heard in a while.

"You want a brownie?" Rachel asked, producing a small plastic container and helping herself.

"My wife made 'em" Walter beamed.

Jessica held up a hand in decline. "No thanks, I don't care for sweets, don't have much of a sweet tooth I guess."

"Well I should get going." Walter said while standing. "I'm supposed to be trying to catch speeders."

Jessica chuckled. "Well, I just wanted to stop in and say hi. I really need to go back to work too." She added.

"It was nice to see you both, thanks for coming by." Rachel said before turning her gaze to Walter. "Tell Georgia 'thanks for the brownies."

"Will do..." Walter said.

"Bye guys."

Rachel waved with her good arm, Jessica and Walter waving back before leaving together.

"Hey Walter?" Jessica said to gain his full attention as they walked toward the elevators. "I need to talk to you..."

"Sure Detective..." Walter said with a smile, both stepping next to a wall of the hallway so as not to obstruct the medical staff.

Jessica took a deep breath before continuing.

"This is important, and it's just between you and me, ok?"

"My lips are sealed." he smiled broadly. "What's wrong?"

Several seconds passed in uncomfortable silence as doubts began to assail Jessica.

Just say it Jessica. Just tell him!

Walter waited quietly. "You can tell me anything..." he said consolingly, placing a hand on her shoulder. "You should know that."

Jessica sullenly cast her gaze toward the floor to her left, finally mustering the courage to say the words. "I found out that someone on the force is on the take..."

She looked up from the floor, a somber expression on her face.

"Someone on the force is helping the Medicine Man."

A heavy silence followed her words, the magnitude of her implications striking Walter hard as his face slid into shock and horror.

"Oh god..." he muttered "How did you find this out?"

"Well, you know that guy that infiltrated the precinct a few days ago?"

"Yeah?"

"Well, he called me..."

Walter's eyes widened as he sputtered a bit to find his voice. "He called you!" He said, looking around afterward in realizing that he may have been too loud.

"Yeah, he told me he found out from Lesco before we caught on to him."

"JEEZ-us." Walter said astonished. "Any idea who it might be?"

"No," Jessica said. "I'm betting Lesco knows though. I'm gonna play a little hard ball with him I think. I need you to do something for me though."

"Sure thing..." Walter said, eager to help.

"I've been trying to figure out who this guy is who got into the station." Jessica continued. "He's a practitioner of Ninjutsu."

"Nin-what...?" Walter said with a puzzled look on his face.

"He's a practitioner of the Ninja's martial arts, the real ninja. Not some movie stunt man."

Walter shook his head in near disbelief. "This is crazy."

"Believe me Walter, this guy is the real deal."

A moment of silence passed between them before Walter replied. "So what do you need from me?"

"Well, I learned that you can't just go into any martial arts school and train in this stuff. It's a very old and unique style. A lot different from Kung-fu or Karate, and a lot less well known. There are a few places in the U.S. that teach it and I did some checking into them."

"What did you find out?" Walter asked eagerly.

"Well the authenticity of a lot of 'em was pretty questionable. Jessica continued. "The few that seemed legitimate though don't teach the espionage aspects of the art to just anyone."

"Espionage?" Walter's brow furrowed. "You mean like a secret agent or a spy or something?"

"Yeah, that's exactly what it is." She said looking at him steadily. "Like I said, it's unique."

"So why do you think this guy wants the Medicine Man.?" Walter asked.

"I think he lost someone close to him."

"And now he wants payback?" Walter inquired.

"Actually, he didn't seem vengeful to me. He was surprisingly composed emotionally, had almost Buddhist calm about him when he spoke to me."

"Ooookay... So where did he learn this Ninjat, to be a Ninja I mean?"

"I think he's been to Japan..." Jessica replied reflectively, almost to herself as she seemed to stare off for a moment. "That's where the art originated from."

She returned her gaze to Walter as she continued.

"I'm gonna gamble on him being someone who's a native to Elmira. I need you to look into airline ticket purchases and such for me, see if you can find anyone from around here that's been to Japan, possibly for a long period of time."

"This is crazy." Walter repeated as they began walking towards the elevators again. "How far are we gonna need to look back here?"

"I would say within the last twenty years or so."

"This is a helluva long shot Jessica."

"I know, but it's our only shot."

Jessica and Walter stopped before an elevator, Walter pressing the down button for them both as they waited.

"Please, not a word of this to anyone." Jessica said, her serious tone reminding Walter of the need for secrecy. "A lot may depend on this."

"My lips are sealed." He repeated as they boarded the empty elevator. Silently they both exited the hospital, stopping briefly beside Walter's squad car.

"Thanks Walter." She finally said. "I really appreciate this, all of it."

"Sure thing..."

"Let me know about anything you find ASAP, ok?"

"Will do. You be careful."

With that Walter entered his car and drove away. Jessica watched as he disappeared into the busy afternoon traffic. Her eyebrows furrowed a reflection of her thoughts.

Ok Lesco, time to find out what you know...

Chapter 11

With a determined stride, Jessica charged through the precinct, several of her fellow officers taking notice of her haste as she rushed by. With seething eyes, she glared at her destination: the entrance to the cell blocks. The door leading to the cells below yielded as she easily pulled it open.

The soles of her sneaker's pounded the concrete steps in her decent, causing the officer at the bottom to look up.

"Detective Devins..." The officer said, seeming surprised.

"Hello Officer Mitchel." she replied. "I wish to speak with Thomas Lesco."

Officer Mitchel produced a clipboard and pen from below the folding chair in which he was seated. "Sign in please."

Jessica knew that as a precautionary attempt to protect Lesco, anyone wishing to see him had to check in before doing so, as well as sign out afterward.

Showing no surprise in her facial expression she snatched the clipboard, proceeding to sign her name, along with the time of her entry after a quick glance at the clock at her back.

"I shouldn't be long..." she said, impatiently handing the clipboard back. Stepping aside, Officer Mitchel motioned for her to go ahead after unlocking the door.

Stepping through the doorway, Jessica's eyes slightly widened in surprise. Her gaze landed on a second officer seated at the beginning of the corridor, a slender black woman with long black hair who quietly read a magazine.

Perfect. Just perfect.

Proceeding past the second guard, Jessica gave a polite nod to her in greeting as she feigned a friendly smile, attempting to mask her annoyance at the woman's presence as best she could.

"Good afternoon Detective Devins."

"Officer Collins..."

Jessica frowned as she proceeded on, knowing full well this was going to hinder things.

No going back now... I gotta figure out something...

Stopping before Lesco's cell, she turned to look inside. He laid contently on the cot. The sight of him resting calmly made her anger flare momentarily.

"Thomas Lesco." She said.

Thomas looked up. "What the hell do you want? I don't have to do nothing until after my court hearing."

"I want to talk."

Thomas sat up frowning. "I've told you guys I don't know who the Medicine Man is." he snapped. "We've been through it all already, so why don't you just piss off and let me relax."

Jessica's eyebrows sloped into a deep furrow, her teeth clenching angrily.

You know who the officer is who runs protection for the Medicine Man, you son of a bitch, and you're gonna tell me who it is!

She could easily imagine herself saying such words, the last of her patience gone as she carried out her interrogations in ways best described as police brutality.

The information regarding the Medicine Man's police connections was desperately needed, and frustratingly unobtainable due to an unforeseen obstruction in the form of a babysitter in police uniform. She glanced toward Officer Collins, who remained involved in her reading.

Shit. I can't say a damn thing in front of her. She could be the one for all I know...

Jessica knew that Officer Collins had been with the force for several years now. She still had no proof even that there was a leak in the precinct, and her secret knowledge had begun to gnaw on her sanity, making her suspicious of everyone. She knew full well that hurling accusations without just cause would cause an internal strife of the worst sort. She would only hurt the investigation, not to mention her working relationship with Officer Collins, and her own career if she was wrong.

Jessica's hands balled into fists, anger and frustration deeply setting in as she turned sharply to storm away. After a few steps she suddenly stopped. Turning her head slightly, she cast her gaze over her shoulder back towards Lesco's cell. Her lips formed an almost malevolent smile as she turned back to renew her efforts.

Okay you lousy piece of gutter trash. We'll see how tough you are.

Stopping before his cell once more, Jessica removed a small notepad and BAL point pen from her jacket pocket. "Are you deaf bitch?" Lesco spat, angrily sitting up once again upon seeing her return. "How many times do I have to..?

"You said you don't know who the Medicine Man is." Jessica interrupted calmly, her eyes locked upon Lesco's with a penetrating stare. "I'm sure you know other things though, like where other suppliers are. Crack houses. Meth labs. I want all the addresses you know, and I want them now."

"Officer!" Lesco called out to Officer Collins, who perked up in alarm.

"Twenty thousand dollars..." Jessica interrupted again. "Isn't that what your bail is set at?"

Lesco suddenly grew quiet, leery of where the conversation was heading.

"A loan with my house as collateral could get that amount." Jessica continued, Officer Collins now approaching. "If you don't want to talk to me, there's no reason for you to be in here living off the tax payers' money."

"C'mon Detective." Officer Collins suggested, attempting to escort her from the cell blocks.

Jessica glared at Officer Collins.

"Please Detective Devins. Come back after you've had a chance to calm down."

"I am calm..." She turned her glare back to Lesco, staring straight in his face.

"Your bail will be paid soon. I'm sure that maniac in the black costume can find you again easily enough. Maybe he'll kill you next time. One less drug dealing punk on the streets is how I see it!"

Thomas' eyes widened in horror as Jessica turned to depart.

"You're bluffing!"

Jessica stopped. Turning to face him once more, she uttered but two more words before continuing on.

"Am I?"

Within seconds, Thomas sprang from his cot. Crashing frantically into his cell bars, he pressed his face between two in order to try to see Jessica. "You're crazy!" he screamed hysterically. "You're fuckin crazy!"

Jessica continued on in silence.

"Alright!" Lesco shouted, causing Jessica to stop before the cell block's exit. "Alright! I'll tell you what you want to know! I'LL FUCKIN TELL YOU!"

Slowly Jessica turned, her lips forming into a grin of victory. She marched back to Lesco's cell, confidence in her stride as Officer Collins looked on. She produced her writing implements once more, the pen giving a satisfying click as she pressed its top with her thumb. Placing the tip to the paper, she eyed Lesco with a smug gaze.

"I'm waiting."

Chapter 12

The sound of an occasional coming or going vehicle called out from the nearby street. The soft singing of birds filled the air with a melodious chorus of gentle chirps. A slight breeze commanded the limbs of trees that dotted the suburbs yards to sway, their leaves creating a rhythm of rustling sounds as the rays of the midday sun poured down from a clear blue sky to give warmth, light and hope to the area.

For the first time in a while, Jessica too, now felt that there was hope, hope for a future in which the city she had sworn to protect was free of the poisons and corruption of the Medicine Man. Dreams of such a utopia danced in her head, the soles of her running shoes battering the pavement as she jogged along the sidewalk, her perspiring form clad in navy blue nylon shorts and a pale blue tank top to accommodate the warmer weather. The lengthy strands of her red hair, usually allowed to flow freely, swung to and fro in a ponytail as she ran.

The Elmira Police Department had made more arrests in the past three weeks than in the entire five years that the Medicine Man investigation had spanned. With the information Jessica had managed to wrest from Thomas Lesco, dealers and distributors where being brought in by the dozens. Every meth-lab and crack house brought down loosened the Medicine Man's hold on the city a little more. It had to be only a matter of time before the mysterious drug lord himself was brought to justice.

Suddenly Jessica halted her run. Staring ahead, she noticed smoke rising in the distance, her thoughts for a brighter tomorrow interrupted as it formed into a billowing tower of blackness against the clear sky.

A fire...

Seeking the source of the blaze, her eyes followed the smoke's trail down to the distant road ahead. A gasp caught in her throat as she spotted the inferno. The familiar flashing of emergency lights covered the street before the burning house as the fire department, police and medical personal were at the scene. Quickly resuming a run, she dashed for the house in the event her assistance would be needed.

She could feel the fire's heat from the street as she arrived, the smell of burning timber assaulting her nose as she surveyed the situation. Several onlookers from neighboring houses had gathered to watch in horror from afar. Gallon after gallon of pressurized water was launched into the conflagration as several men in firefighter gear manned the thick hose. A thunderous explosion from within the home forced gasps and screams from the on looking crowd, the fire fighters ducking as shards of glass erupted from the windows of the two story house.

As the battle to stop the fire's destruction continued, a commotion amid the officers and fireman grabbed Jessica's attention. Her ears caught the screams and pleas of a frantic woman, urgent cries that brought forth a terrible realization.

"My son! My son is upstairs! Please! My son!" The woman sobbed hysterically as she was restrained by a man in firefighting gear.

Oh my God!

Jessica watched as a policeman assisted the firefighter, taking hold of the crazed woman and pulling her back in an attempt to save her life. "The place is gonna come down!" The firefighter screamed. "I can't let you go in there!"

Turning her gaze back to the burning house, Jessica could hear the roar of the flame. Strained support beams groaned, threatening to let the roof collapse at any moment. Then, barely audible over the inferno's rage, she heard it: The horrified screams of a child within.

Her heart began to race. She looked at the anguished mother once again, authorities continuing to hold her back as she punished her raw throat with deafening screams for someone to help; for the men to release her as she reached for the building with an outstretched arm as if she could reach it to save her little boy. A sense of hesitancy crept into Jessica's mind as she returned her gaze to the house, fear flooding her as she came to terms with what must be done. If no one tried to get the boy out now, he would die.

Mustering all her inner resolve and courage, she broke into a full sprint. Blowing past several police officers and firefighters, she rushed for the house, authorities unable to stop her in her unexpected passing. Ignoring the yells for her to stop, she charged through the front doorway as black smoke rolled out of the house from every opening.

The inside of the dwelling was like a furnace, the walls seeming to be made of flames as all around was engulfed. Blistering heat caused her exposed flesh to cry in agony as she quickly began to choke on the heavy smoke filled air. Coughing, she lowered herself to a crouching position as her hand reflexively covered her mouth. Her now streaming eyes burned as she quickly swung her head about, incredible presence of mind allowing her to remember that the boy was on the upper floor of the house as she frantically searched for a flight of stairs.

"Where are you?" She called out loudly in frantic hope to hear a reply.

Please God...

Above her, she suddenly heard the loud breaking of timber. Reflexively diving aside, she barely avoided a portion of the ceiling as it came down in a fiery mass, embers flying as the debris crashed to the floor. Struggling, she pushed herself to her hands and knees, her ears again catching the boy's cries as they rose above the roar of the flames. "I'm coming!" She cried out in response, scrambling towards the hysterical screams. "Hold on!"

Making her way through the smoke, Jessica continued toward the sounds of the boy, soon managing to find the base of a rising stairway. Forcing herself to her feet, she cast her gaze up toward its apex, the screams appearing to come from an alcove above. With the aid of a railing at her left, she began to rush toward the top. "I'm coming!"

As she neared the landing, she suddenly felt her footing leave her, the stairwell collapsing without warning. Screaming, she desperately reached out for anything to stop her fall, barely managing to catch herself on the alcove's ledge as the stairs crashed many feet below her. Hanging on for her life, her arms quivered as she struggled to muscle herself up onto the ledge, her grasp on the ledge insufficient to lift her weight. Slowly, she could feel her fingers begin to slip from the hard wood ledge as she dangled helplessly. She knew she was going to fall.

No!

Jessica screamed as her fingers finally slipped free. She was sure that the fall would render her unable to escape the house. She too would die, along with the boy she had come to save.

Without warning, her decent into a fiery oblivion was abruptly halted, as she felt what could only be the hand of another firmly grip her right wrist. Raising her gaze up from the fire below, her eyes met that of the one who was her rescuer.

"I have you Jessica." The ninja said reassuringly, his voice calm amid the hell around him.

Resting on his stomach, his right arm served as additional support for both Jessica's weight and his own. From his left arm she hung as it extended over the ledge at the shoulder, his position clearly indicating that he had dove to save her. As the muscles in his arms tensed, he began to lift her up onto the landing while getting his knees beneath him. With her free hand, Jessica grabbed the ledge once again to aid her rescuer's attempts as she was hauled safely onto the landing through their combined efforts. With grateful eyes Jessica stared, as though momentarily entranced, at her savior.

He looked in every way as she had imagined, based on descriptions given by those already in police custody. Clad entirely in black, he wore the traditional V-neck jacket, trousers and split-toed footwear worn so long ago by the ninja of old that she had researched. The lower portion of his arms and the back of his gloved hands were shielded by a protective armor. The hood and mask which veiled his face allowed only his eyes to be seen.

The cracking of strained support beams overhead caused Jessica and the ninja to glance upwards. The scream of the boy shot through them both, terror filled and piercing as it came from down the hallway. Jessica looked over her shoulder to the doorway that the cries seemed to be coming from.

"You have to get him out now!" The ninja yelled above the roar, his voice urgent.

Standing quickly, Jessica ran to the closed door of what she assumed was the boy's room. A quick glance back allowed her to see the ninja one more time as he charged toward the alcove's opposite end, his form quickly vanishing behind the thick smoke and burning debris that fell around him. Turning back to the door, she felt the handle gingerly to see if flame waited on the other side.

Warm, but not hot, should be safe to open.

She turned the handle and pushed into the room, quickly spotting the boy. She guessed him to be no more than six years of age as he sat upon the floor, his back pressed firmly against the side of a race-car shaped bed. Soot stained his white t-shirt and matching shorts, black smoke marks marring his round face. Tear tracks cut through the stains on his face as he sobbed continuously, sweaty and exhausted from bawling as Jessica scooped him up from the floor, his weight enough to make her groan slightly from her already tired arms.

With the boy's arms around her neck and his face hid in her shoulder, she lost no time in running to a shattered window that was but a few feet away. The boy's legs wrapped tightly around her waist; his little body still shuttering with sobs as he clung to her in a terrified hug. Looking out, she could see the front yard below, the fireman still scrambling about in their war with the blaze as several onlookers and policemen pointed to her location in the window with astonished gasps and exclamations. Another crashing sound caused her to instinctively toss a glance behind her. More of the house had collapsed, the hallway she had left now a ruin of burning timber and flame that left her trapped in the boy's room, the window their only hope of escape.

Turning her attention back to the crowd below, she saw several firefighters running towards the section of lawn below their window, synchronizing their movements to form a ring with a canvas tarp they held between them which they pulled taught.

"Hurry!" She screamed, again glancing to her back. Visibility in the room was quickly reaching zero. Holding the sobbing boy tightly around his back, she stepped up onto the windows edge, pulling herself up with her free hand.

With her last ounce of strength, she leaped from the window, aiming for the canvas in which the firefighters had ready to break her fall. The descent seemed like an eternity, a pulling sensation in her gut as she tightly held her eyes shut. Upon landing on her seat and back without injury, her eyes quickly flashed open again as she realized she had landed on the yielding surface of the outstretched canvas, many hands helping her to regain her footing. Urgent cries of "Go!" "Hurry!" And "Get back!" could be heard all around her as she carried the boy swiftly away from the burning home.

Sighs of relief and cheers filled the air before being drowned out by the deafening roar of the collapsing house, a brilliant flare of flying embers and billowing smoke reaching many feet into the air. Jessica was soon surrounded, people pressing into her with praises of her valor and courage while she tiredly handed the boy to his mother. Tears of joy streamed down the woman's face as she eagerly took her son, still crying as she held him close.

"God bless you!"

Jessica only managed a weak smile in reply before being urged towards a nearby ambulance by a medic. "Let's get you checked out hero..."

Hero. It wasn't a title she felt she alone deserved, for she and the boy would both be dead if it wasn't for the aid of another, one who apparently had been unseen by all but her. A flash of worry erupted through her. She herself had been fortunate to sustain only minor burns, and she hoped that her rescuer had also escaped the house more or less unscathed. She rested quietly on the back of an ambulance, tanks onboard providing her O2 that she gratefully took in through a face mask held over her nose and mouth.

"I'll be back to check on you in a few minutes..." the medic said reassuringly before departing to assist others.

Several minutes passed as Jessica took slow, deep breaths to replenish her oxygen starved body, frantic activity all around her as she recuperated from her ordeal. As she sat, she suddenly noticed something out of the corner of her eye. Turning her head slowly, she spotted the ninja atop the roof of a house across the street.

A sense of relief washed over her as she slowly stood. Unconsciously, she lowered the oxygen mask from her mouth. Her eyes locked on the dark figure in amazement as he held a crouching position, seeming almost majestic as he watched events unfold.

At that moment, she began to realize that this man was more, much more than a vigilante that her department sought to arrest. He was a light, one of the few now remaining in a city which was blanketed in darkness.

In a place and time were some among the law worked to aid society's evils; could such a man be the only way to bring justice and peace once more?

The circumstances that put him in opposition to her as an officer of the law caused a sense of sadness in her, as she now realized without a doubt what it was that the ninja strived for. Continuing to stare in near amazement, Jessica whispered but two words. "Thank you."

The ninja turned his gaze to her, giving a single nod of his head as if in acknowledgment before deftly turning to disappear over the edge of the slanted rooftop. Jessica's stare remained on the spot he had stood, her lips slowly beginning to show hints of a smile ready to form.

Hero.

Chapter 13

ho are you? Where are you?
Questions regarding the mysterious ninja's identity and whereabouts continued to beg for answers as Jessica stared out through her living room window. The night beyond her front yard seemed endless in contrast to the lights along the street, casting soft pools of illumination down from their positions. Houses and trees around the neighborhood were blanketed in shadows. Lights from within some of the homes gave off a soft glow from behind curtained windows, as a full moon shined brightly against the dark, yet clear sky.

A sigh escaped her as she turned away from the view, never before feeling so torn. Her interest in the ninja no longer bared any similarity with that of a police officer's in a criminal and their motivations. She didn't want to bring this man to justice as she would any other who broke the law. She wanted to *know* this man, to hold in her heart what he did, and to believe as he did.

Sitting upon the sofa, she grabbed the book acquired from the library, taking it from atop the coffee table as she turned to rest her back against the sofa's armrest. Extending her legs along the length of the couch, she allowed her bare feet to hang over the edge of the opposite armrest while crossing her ankles in a comfortable posture. She opened the book at a place she had marked with a folded piece of paper, continuing to read where she had previously left off.

Several quiet minutes were spent perusing the contents of the chapter before she suddenly halted her reading. Her gaze rose from the book's text as a nagging feeling tugged at her, the feeling that someone was behind her. Slowly she turned her head, twisting her torso to better see as she looked over her right shoulder. Standing there with piercing eyes that cast a steely gaze down at her from behind a black mask, was the Ninja, his arms folded sternly across his chest as he stood silent and imposing.

Jessica quickly jerked up to a seated position, her eyes flashing open as she let out a startled shriek. Twisting in her seat on the sofa, she glanced about in paranoia. A sigh escaped her parted lips as she realized that she was the only one there.

Great, now I'm dreaming about him...

All remained as she remembered it prior to her apparent and accidental dozing off, the book on ninjutsu that she had been reading laying open in her lap. With a groan she closed the book, dropping it onto the coffee table to land with a sharp thud. Resting her feet upon the floor, she leaned forward, her elbows coming to rest atop her legs above the knees as she buried her face in the palms of her hands. Several seconds passed in this manner as Jessica quietly collected herself.

I gotta stop doing this. I'm becoming obsessed with this guy.

The sudden ringing of her telephone interrupted the silence, causing her to groan in slight annoyance as she turned to take the call.

"Hello?"

"Good evening Detective." The voice of Walter replied from the other end in his usually upbeat manner.

"Hey Walter..." Jessica yawned, fatigue settling back on her.

"Did I wake you?" Walter asked, noticing the grogginess in her voice.

"It's okay, I just dozed off a bit..."

"Sorry 'bout waking you," he replied apologetically. "but I got some good news."

"Oh?" Jessica said as she massaged her forehead lightly with her fingertips, skepticism evident in her voice.

"I think I found your ninja..."

Jessica's eyes widened as Walter's incredible statement seemed to hang in the air before her. Her every action ceased as she seemed to freeze mid movement, her attention hanging on Walter's every word as her body slid slowly to the edge of the couch in anticipation.

"You ever met a guy named Clayton Drake?"

Jessica paused for a moment. "No. I can't say I have."

"Well," Walter continued. "I got a friend in Elmira's FBI office to give me a hand and help look into those flight records like you requested. We found one under his name, along with a travel Visa. He took a trip to Japan about twelve years ago."

Walter paused a moment, the sound of paper rustling on his end. "I did a background check on this guy. He currently works for the Elmira Star."

"The local paper?" Jessica said in shock. She quickly reached under her coffee table where she retrieved several past copies of the city's daily publication.

"Yup." Walter continued on into her silence. "As it turns out though, prior to that he was a photographer for *National Geographic Magazine*."

Jessica quickly flipped through one of the newspapers while tilting her head to securely hold the phone's receiver between her head and shoulder. Her eyes widened as she found what she was looking for, slowly taking the phone receiver in her hand once more as she stared at the article's headline.

Unexpected Death Hinders Medicine Man Investigation. Clayton Drake

"He wrote the article in the paper that covered Robert Kane's death." she said aloud, as much to herself as to Walter.

"That one among others." Walter added "He returned to Japan again after his first assignment trip, and this is the kicker.... He was over there on a work Visa for about ten years before returning home about a year ago."

"Jesus." Jessica said under her breath. "Ten years?"

"Oh it gets better Detective," Walter said. "think I found a motive too."

Jessica stood, making her way to her living room window. "Go on." she urged while staring out into the night.

"Well, do you remember a teenage boy named Randy Kent?" Walter inquired.

"Randy Kent?" she said, pondering the name. "It sounds familiar."

"It should. The boy died of a drug overdose about a year ago. In our investigation we found WET in his room."

"Marijuana soaked in formaldehyde for the opium derivative." Jessica said with a frown. "It gets its name from the glossy sheen it has after its dried. It causes a powerful high and is murderously addictive."

"You know your narcotics Detective." Walter said. "As it turns out though, that boy was Clayton Drake's nephew. We know some of the Medicine Man's people sell that crap. Sounds to me like your ninja came home to find this guy himself."

Jessica stared off in silence, her mind working furiously.

"You still there Detective?"

"Uh yeah... Listen, you haven't told anyone else about this, have you?"

"I told you, *my lips are sealed.*" Walter replied, with a smile evident in his voice.

Jessica sighed audibly in relief.

"I suppose you want his address and my notes so you can get a warrant?" Walter continued.

"Actually..." Jessica began. "Hold off on that for the moment. I need you to sit on this for now, I'm not sure I'm ready act on it yet. I also don't want him to know that I'm on to him."

"So?" Walter started, a note of perplexion in his voice. "What now?"

"Can you get the address to the Kents for me?"

"Sure, you mean the boy's parents right? Gimme a lil' bit and I can get it."

Jessica quickly found a pen and waited to write on a corner of the newsprint.

The headlights of Jessica's car pierced the darkness ahead as she brought the Impalla slowly to a stop at the streets curb. Shutting off the headlights and engine, she glanced at the piece of folded paper that now had the address of the Kents scrawled on it.

Hope I won't be interrupting anything.

She glanced at her watch, seeing the time to be five minutes past eight P.M. Exiting the vehicle, she began making her way up a cement block sidewalk that lead to the Kent family's home.

The crème colored two-story ranch-style home stood proudly. The yard was very well maintained, with the show of a flower garden beginning to bloom under the front windows at the approach of warmer weather. A whitewashed wooden porch with an overhanging roof and a pleasant looking two-seater swing that hung from its supports greeted Jessica as she stepped up to a metal front door. A white framed window set into it with a flower pattern curtain that hung up in a country style tie off down the center. A brown carpeted mat was at her feet, black letters to spell *Welcome* and several yellow sunflowers embroidered into it. This was clearly a home for what had once been a happy family. Jessica couldn't help but feel a pang of sadness at the thought of their tragedy.

With the index finger of her right hand, she gently pressed the small round button located near the front door. The ringing of the doorbell could easily be heard as it called to the residents inside.

Patiently, she waited as she heard a voice pleasantly call out from inside. "Coming." The sound of footsteps sounded softly from behind the door.

Jessica could see the silhouette of a person before the front porch light was turned on and the door opened. A middle-aged woman stood in front of her, just across the thresh-hold. Just over five feet in height and wearing house shoes, the woman looked at her with a politely puzzled appearance in her gentle eyes. Her hair was cut neat in a paige boy which was slightly out of date, the blond tresses showing signs of age with silvery gray strands near her temples and throughout the length.

"Yes? May I help you?"

"Mrs. Kent?" Jessica asked rhetorically. "I'm Detective Devins of the Elmira Police Department. May I have a little of your time?"

忍

"Sugar?" Mrs. Kent offered politely as she poured tea for her guest.

"No thank you." Jessica declined with a polite smile as she was handed her saucer and cup. A pleasant smell emanated from the steaming liquid as her host seated herself, caddy-corner from Jessica in a recliner that matched her own seat. Jessica sipped cautiously at the hot tea, unsure of what to say from here. She wondered if Mrs. Kent even knew that her brother was a suspected vigilante, guessing not from the woman's calm and kind demeanor. Seconds passed tensely as the silence stretched.

"Is your husband home, Mrs. Kent?" Jessica finally asked, trying to keep a lighthearted casualness in her visit.

"No." Mrs. Kent replied, sitting back comfortably in her chair. "He works second shift. He won't be home 'till midnight."

"I see." Jessica said, unsure of what to say next.

"Have there been any new leads in the Medicine Man Case, Detective Devins?" Mrs. Kent asked easily. Jessica was relieved inwardly as she placed her saucer and cup on the coffee table before answering.

"We believe we are close to catching him, ma'am." she replied, glad for the brief levity of her tension.

Jessica's stomach tightened as she continued. "I know this past year has been very difficult for you and your husband. I couldn't begin to imagine what you have been going through, and I want to thank you both for all the help you have given us in the investigation." Mrs. Kent nodded slowly, clearly trying to fight back the memory of her loss. "I was wondering if you knew of anyone else who might be able to help us. Maybe offer us more information." Jessica continued, trying to steer the conversation carefully to what she was really here for without giving herself away. "I mean, someone else who must have been close to Randy, a friend or family member that we may have overlooked. We were extensive in our leads, but I was wondering if there might have been anyone else."

As Jessica took a sip of her tea, she looked over the rim of her cup, her gaze suddenly landing on a framed photograph on the wall across from her. Amid a collection of other family photos on the wall, was a picture of Randy with another man. She realized it wasn't his father from other photos.

"Well." Mrs. Kent pondered as Jessica studied the picture.

Holding fishing poles, the duo stood, smiling happily for the camera. With tackle boxes piled at their feet, the pair stood side by side with a lake at their backs, its surface smooth and calm as a wooden deck stretched out into the water, several small boats tied to it. Wearing khaki shorts, sandals, and a hunter green t-shirt, the slender yet muscular man had his arm around the young Randy's shoulders, the boy holding up for the camera a large mouth bass of moderate size, a catch the boy seemed to be very proud off.

Jessica focused, mentally forming the visual of a black mask to cover the man's face. She recognized the eyes from previous encounters, eyes that clearly showed a love for the boy as well as a love for life itself.

That's him! It has to be!

"I'm not really sure who else you could talk to Detective." Mrs. Kent said, breaking Jessica's thoughts. "I told the police all about his friends that I knew of."

"Yes, we have gleaned all we can from them I think." Jessica answered, turning her head back to her hostess. "What about other family?"

"Well, besides me and his father, he was very close to my brother Clayton. They spent a lot of time together when Clayton came around. But I'm not sure what more he could tell you about where Randy could have gotten... where he got the drugs."

Jessica listened in silence, her eyes glancing back to the photos for a moment. "That wouldn't be him there, would it?" she asked innocently, with a casual nod of her head directed toward the photo.

"Yes that's him." Mrs. Kent replied. "He's younger than me and he liked the outdoors. He and Randy used to spend a lot of time together in the summer. They both loved to go fishing together. Of course, it was always up to me to clean and cook it." A sad smile played across Mrs. Kent's face as she looked fondly at the photo. "They were very close. My brother's always been really sweet."

Jessica continued to gaze at the picture. "I'd very much like to speak with him."

"I could give you his address if you'd like?" Mrs. Kent volunteered.

Jessica smiled. "That would be great," she said with a strange combination of feigned and sincere gratitude, as she secretly already had access to the address. Patiently, she waited as Mrs. Kent wrote the address down for her.

"Thank you so much for your time Mrs. Kent," Jessica said, "and for the tea. It was very good."

"Of course." Mrs. Kent smiled. "It was pleasant having company. Thank you for coming."

Jessica took the slip of paper that Mrs. Kent offered. "I really appreciate this." she added gently. *More than you could possibly know...*

Chapter 14

Jessica closed the door behind her upon entering her home. The sharp click of the latch ended the stillness that had permeated prior to her return. With a somber look on her face, she removed her shoes to leave them by the door before making her way toward the comfort of her sofa. With an emotional fatigue in her eyes, she seated herself with an exhausted flop.

Leaning back in her seat, her gaze naturally fixed on the ceiling as her head came to rest comfortably on the back of the couch. Sighing deeply, she closed her eyes. Guilt churned in her stomach as she prepared to make the most difficult choice of her career.

Her gaze turned toward her telephone. She had all the evidence necessary to launch an investigation. It was only a matter of placing a call to the station and requesting a search warrant. A thorough search of Clayton Drake's home would surely reveal him to be the ninja. She only needed to make the call.

Deep down, she knew it was a call she wouldn't, *couldn't*, make. In a matter of days, one man had helped her accomplish more than the police had accomplished in five years. The fact that she was as close as she was to finding the Medicine Man, the fact that she knew about the corruption among her own, and the fact that she was still alive to continue this struggle, she owed it all to the actions of one man.

It wasn't a vigilante, or a man who merely sought some sort of retribution or personal gratification, who aided her so much. It was a man who understood what justice truly was. It was the same belief that she and her father both shared.

Jessica's mind returned to the night of her father's death, the night that had haunted her since its transpiration. She sat at her father's bedside in the Arnot Ogden Hospital, gently holding his hand in her own as she looked at him with teary eyes. He was the strongest man she had known, and he had fought a long time with his wound, nearly a week. "The bastard who did this is going to pay," she whispered, her voice clearly stained with malice. "I swear to God I'll get him Dad."

Her father had managed a weak, compassionate smile through his haze of pain as he looked up at her fondly.

"Don't mistake revenge for justice, Jessica." He said. "You should never seek to deal out punishment in an attempt to make yourself feel better." He coughed before continuing. "Justice is about balance and harmony. It's what you, as a police officer, have sworn to maintain. Never forget that, sweetheart."

Tears ran freely down Jessica's cheeks.

"Dad."

"I love you, baby."

Those words would be his last, a few more shaky breaths escaped before the continuous high pitched hum of a flat-lined heart monitor filled the room.

"I love you too, Daddy."

A single tear trickled down Jessica's cheek at the painful memory.

I love you.

She still wished she had uttered those words sooner, words that would have mattered much more than any spoken vow of vengeance. In his final moments however, he had done all in his power to ensure that his daughter truly understood justice. She now knew that the ninja had this same understanding. Beneath the mask, was a man like her father.

Through her brief conversation with him over the phone, as well as her talk with his sister, Jessica understood that an emotional composure unlike any imaginable by her guided this man's actions, not any desire to destroy. No real harm had come to any of the men that he had apprehended, despite the potential lethality of his skills. His compassion clearly separated him from any anguish-consumed lunatic, as well as from those that he fought against.

A thin line separated 'legal' and 'right' and Jessica now knew on which side of that line she stood. The man had done all he could to help her, warning her about her corrupt colleagues, even risking his own life to save her from a burning house. These were things of honor. Things that were right. He was not obligated to do any of these things, but he had done them, and turning him over to those who were secretly serving a greater evil would serve injustice. Her decision was final. The apprehension of the Ninja , of Clayton Drake, would be an affair that she would play no part in.

A knock at the door suddenly jerked Jessica back from her thoughts. "Who is it?" she called out from her seat on the couch, wiping her teary eyes on the back of her hand.

"It's Officer Mitchel." a reply came from behind her front door.

David Mitchel?

She recognized the officer's voice, detecting a sense of urgency in it as she lifted herself from the couch and went to the front door.

"I really need to talk to you Jessica. It's important." Opening the door a quarter of the way, she stood just across its threshold. "I really hope I'm not bothering you, Jessica." David continued, now that she stood before him. His voice was wary and constrained, clearly shaken. "I didn't know who else I could turn to."

Jessica pondered the nature of David's sudden visit, figuring he must have looked up her address at the station. She wondered if he had stumbled across something involving what she already knew about the police corruption. It was the only thing she could think of that would leave the young officer so distressed. That being the case, this was the chance she was waiting for. With viable evidence, she could put a stop to the corruption and bring the Medicine Man to justice. There also was another possibility, the thought of which caused her sudden panic and paranoia. David could be involved with the Medicine Man. He could be here to kill her.

Jessica scanned the area beyond David as discreetly as possible. Her yard and the street around seemed deserted. Only her neighbor's familiar vehicles and David's own car were to be seen. *Nothing suspicious anywhere.* It seemed he had come alone.

"Have you been crying?" he asked, sounding somewhat concerned.

"Forget about it David." she replied abruptly before opening the door fully and stepping aside. "Come on in." She scanned the area for signs of treachery one last time as David entered her house.

It's a risk I gotta take.

She closed the door, fastening the bolt home as David walked a little ways into her living room. She could see the tension in him as he turned to face her, a man clearly on edge. His hands trembled slightly. Each breath was nervous as his eyes looked to the floor.

"Can I get you something to drink?" she offered, hoping to calm him. "Coffee or something?"

"No thank you." he declined, politely removing his police hat while looking up at her.

Jessica approached him, placing a comforting hand on his shoulder as she stood in front of him, her eyes level with his, as he wasn't a tall man.

"Calm down ok? You can talk to me, David." she said reassuringly.

David nodded, taking a few deep breaths as he seemed to relax a bit.

"Alright," she began anew, "now tell me what this is about."

"I'm not sure how to begin." David replied softly. "It's about the Chief."

Jessica's heart began to sink. She already suspected what he was about to tell her as he silently worked up the resolve needed to continue.

"I think the Chief... I think he is running protection for the Medicine Man."

Her eyes widened in horror. If this where true, things where even worse than she thought. The moment seemed to hang between them forever, statement resounding in her ears.

"How do you know?" she finally asked, breaking the silence.

"Well." David began, taking a short pause before he was able to continue. "I had noticed that he had been going down to the cell blocks. I saw him talking to Thomas Lesco, like hush-hush kinda talking. I could never hear what was being said."

Jessica frowned.

"Go on..."

"Besides that," David continued. "The Chief has been getting these letters in the mail. They're addressed to him at the station, but there's no return address, and they're just in regular business envelopes. I just wondered what was going on, so I went through the Chief's desk one afternoon when he was out for lunch. I found this..."

Jessica watched expectantly as David dug into the pocket of his trousers with his right hand. Her breath caught in her throat as she realized what David was withdrawing from his pocket was no letter or paper. In his hand was some sort of shaft, a black metal tube. She blanched as a sudden flick of the wrist ejected a series of interlocking metal bars from their housing. A gasp escaped her as the business end of a collapsible baton suddenly came towards her head.

Barely having time to react, Jessica quickly ducked to avoid the incoming blow. Rising quickly, she swung her right arm outward in a circular motion, her hand intercepting a second attack in the form of back swing. Her hand's edge struck home against David's arm with a knife hand block, just below the wrist. Her left arm soon followed, shooting across to her right side to come up beneath David's still outstretched arm, catching his wrist between her two hands as their positioning formed a 'V' shape.

Continuing to swing her left arm up with a circular motion, she effortlessly lifted David's arm, guiding it over and around to her left side while simultaneously withdrawing her right hand to position for a counter strike. Shooting her free arm out, she connected with a back fist to her attacker's temple. The blow stunned David causing him to unconsciously release his grip on the baton.

Pressing the attack, Jessica executed a circular kick with her left leg, the force of the blow jerking David's head violently to her right as the top of her foot struck hard against the side of his jaw. Spinning around from the momentum of her attack, she executed a second circular kick, bringing her right leg up and around to blast his jaw again with the heel of her foot.

David spun around from the force of the kicks, staggering away from Jessica several feet before falling to the floor on all fours. She held a ready position and watched David favor his jaw with his right hand, signs of swelling already becoming evident.

"So," Jessica began with a frown. "You're the one the Medicine Man has under his thumb. You must have spent some time rehearsing that bit about the chief. Your anxiety even seemed pretty genuine. I guess treachery really works on your nerves huh David?"

No reply came as David struggled to one knee.

"I guess it's a good thing I have quick reflexes." Jessica continued. You almost had me. Since you're obviously the one working for the Medicine Man, I'd say it's a safe guess that you not only know who he is, but where he is, and this is information that you're going to share with me and the rest of the force."

Jessica jerked up in alarm as she heard her back door suddenly burst open from in her kitchen. Quickly entering the doorway between her living room and kitchen was Officer Patricia Collins, a pistol in her hands quickly turned on Jessica.

"Don't move!"

"Patricia?"

"Turn around Jessica, and place your hands behind your back." she ordered while aiming a gun from several feet away.

Jessica swallowed, her throat cracking dryly, as she forced down a lump that formed in her throat. Fear began to grip her. Patricia was out of reach, one wrong move and she could easily be dead. David hadn't come alone after all. She wondered how many others on the police force were a part of this.

Her heart sank as she slowly turned her back to Patricia, reluctance evident as she placed her hands to her back in surrender. She could hear hard footsteps coming towards her. Her heart began to race. Sweat beaded on her forehead as Patricia closed in. A slight turning of her head to accommodate the use of her peripheral vision allowed her to see Patricia extract a plastic zip tie from her pocket.

They want me alive?

She knew that if she resisted that she could die. If she allowed her capture, she was sure to die.

Only one chance at this.

Jessica quickly dodged to her right side while simultaneously pivoting on her foot to face Patricia, the motion carrying her safely out of the gun's sight for a moment as she swept her right hand out with a circular motion. Grabbing Patricia's wrist to safely secure the pistol, she sent her left fist in, sending the other woman rocking back as the blow struck her in the mouth. Moving with lightning speed, she grabbed the top of Patricia's hand with her own left while shifting the grip of her right to hold the firearm at the bottom.

Firmly grasping the hand in a claw like grip, with the tips of both thumbs driven hard into its back, Jessica raised Patricia's arm above her. With a quick pivot to her left, she guided the arm around, aiming the palm of her attacker's hand downward while bending it at the wrist. Patricia cried out in pain as the inward wrist lock relieved her of the gun while forcing her on to her back.

Out of the corner of her eyes, Jessica suddenly noticed David as he got to his feet and charged in. Before she could securely ready the pistol, he slammed into her. Her breath was knocked out of her chest as they both fell to the floor, the gun flying out of her grasp and bouncing to a stop under her coffee table.

Jessica squirmed desperately against David's wiry strength. Managing to get behind her in the struggle, David tightly wrapped his arms around her midsection as she successfully fought her way to her feet. Firmly gripping her attacker's arms, Jessica lifted her right leg while bending it at the knee and drove the heel of her sock clad foot into David's instep. His screams of pain were deafening in her ear as he released her to grab at the throbbing foot.

Suddenly, Jessica felt a powerful blow against the back of her neck. Incapacitating pain erupted through her as she crumpled to the floor, agony traveling up and down her neck and spine like electricity through a wire. Almost oblivious to everything around her, she was unable to react as she felt something push roughly against her side. With clouded vision, she barely recognized Patricia's form standing over her, the heel of her foot being used to roll Jessica onto her back. Firmly grasped in her left hand, was the forgotten baton. It was the last thing Jessica saw before her consciousness abandoned her.

The end of the cigarette flared brilliantly in the darkness as the man smoking it took a long drag, smoke filling the air in billowing clouds before him as he exhaled. All was still in the city streets beyond the alleyway in which he stood. Casually, he leaned against the driver's side of a gray SUV, the back window to his left rolled half way down to reveal another figure seated within the rear seat's shadowy interior. A digital ringing from the pocket of the man's pants suddenly called for his attention as he took another drag from his cigarette.

Extracting a cellular phone from his pocket, the man flipped it open to answer the call.

"Yeah?"

In silence he stood listening to the individual on the other end, his lips shaping into a smile as he closed the phone and returned it to his pocket.

The man turned his gaze to the one in the back seat of the car. "They have her." he said. "They're on their way to the rendezvous point now." From within the car's dark interior came the voice of a man, his tone malevolent as he spoke but one word in reply.

"Good..."

The man dropped the finished cigarette upon the pavement after one final drag from it. Casually, he extinguished the smoking butt by stamping down onto it with the ball of his foot before entering the vehicle. The engine of the SUV came to life before driving off, leaving the shadows of the alleyway in which it had been parked behind as it sped down the eerily quiet street, none of those riding in its confines aware of the dark figure that clung to it from underneath as it traveled on.

Chapter 15

Jessica's eyes slowly fluttered open, a low moan creeping from her as she began to regain consciousness. Her head still throbbing dully, she gradually started to stir, still unaware of her surroundings.

Where am I?

Her thoughts came to an abrupt halt as she suddenly noticed that her movements were severely restricted. A startled gasp escaped her as she came to a frightening realization. She had been restrained.

Lying on her side, she quickly began checking herself. Her hands had been zip tied behind her. She could feel the plastic strip dig sharply into her skin as she struggled to free her wrists. Care had also been taken to bind her feet in a similar manner as a zip tie tightly entrapped her ankles.

Now fully in panic's grasp, her struggles became more frantic. Seconds passed, fear flooding her as continued efforts to escape proved to be futile. Desperation urged her to scream for help. It was an urge that she resisted, as she was certain that any cries of distress would go unheard by all but those who had taken her prisoner.

Calm down. You have to calm down.

Twisting about as best she could to look around, she began to get a bearing on her surroundings. Noticing that she lay upon a mere dirt floor, her eyes began adjusting to the darkness. She was soon able to make out the walls around her, their composition seeming to be a heavy sheet metal, with a ceiling several feet above of the same material. Beams of sturdy wood served as framework and supports for the enclosure, leaving her to surmise that the structure in which she had been placed was some sort of abandoned shed.

Ahead of her, the complete absence of one wall permitted her to see the grounds outside her confines. A full moon shined brightly against the night sky, its pale light revealing old expired vehicles of varying makes and models. Other assorted automobile parts lay scattered about the grounds in stacks and mounds, enabling her to deduce where it was that her captors had taken her.

A salvage yard.

Jessica suddenly perked up, blanching as her ears caught the sounds of ongoing conversation and approaching footfalls.

They're coming!

Her eyes widened in fear, the sounds drawing closer as panic embraced her once more. Her heart pounded as she renewed her attempts to escape her bonds, the shifting links of the chains creating sounds that she knew would alert her captors to her frantic struggles.

Officers David Mitchell and Patricia Collins soon stepped into view, their advance followed by that of another, an individual who Jessica instantly recognized. Her eyes widened in as much shock as horror upon seeing the man, her attempts to escape gradually slowing to a stop as she stared in near disbelief.

No.

"I see that you are finally awake, Detective Devins." Chief Higgins cooed with a sinister looking grin. "I hope you are comfortable."

"So you *are* on the take." Jessica finally managed to say.

"Looks like I was telling you the truth after all, huh?" David chimed in. "Can't say that I didn't warn you."

Jessica's eyebrows sloped into a deep furrow, her eyes angrily remaining locked on the chief. "So you've been a part of this all along?" She inquired rhetorically, the question sounding more like a statement. "I guess being a backstabbing son of a bitch pays more huh?" Chief Higgins chuckled slightly, as if amused by Jessica's comments.

"Crime is a good career choice." He said. "It has a lot to offer."

The sound of an approaching vehicle suddenly grabbed the attention of all within the shed, the gaze of the chief and his accomplices turning in unison towards its entrance. Jessica held her breath in fearful anticipation as she heard the opening and closing of multiple automobile doors. Approaching footsteps soon followed.

A group of five men entered the shed. All were clad in casual wear save one, an older man in a charcoal gray Armani suit. Jessica guessed the man to be in or nearing his sixties as he stopped to stand before her, his neatly parted hair thinning and grey. The skin of his hands and visage appeared worn and leathery in his aging, his tired looking eyes gazing down at her as his lips shaped into an ominous grin. "Detective Jessica Devins I presume." the man said, his voice bearing a gruff timber.

Jessica shifted in discomfort against her bonds. Trying to hide her fear, she stared up at the tower of a man; suddenly recognizing of who it was that now loomed over her.

"Rolland Sinclair, you're The Medicine Man." She finally managed to askwith a measure of courage.

"Very good," the man replied. "A detective to the last."

Jessica frowned.

"You may call me Rolland if you like though Detective or Mr. Sinclair if you prefer the usage of formalities."

Jessica found disbelief assailing her.

Rolland Sinclair.

The owner of several local businesses within the city was a pillar of the community, and something of a real estate guru as well. He was known for generous donations to the Elmira Police Department, as well as to other charity organizations on several occasions. She had never actually met the man however, until now.

"Rolland Sinclair began to pace back and forth in front of her in a casual manner, his hands behind him with the right gently grasped in the left as he continued. "It is good to know that the money I have previously donated to your department has been well spent on such fine officers as yourself. I am really quite impressed."

"What are you going to do with me?" Jessica asked, her concerns clearly evident. She surmised that her captors weren't planning to kill her, at least not yet. Sinclair's men could have carried out an execution in her home if that had been their intentions. There had to be another reason for her abduction. "Why did you bring me here?"

"I'm glad you asked, Detective." Stopping before her once more, Sinclair lowered himself to one knee. "You have caused me quite a bit of trouble," he started, "I could very easily kill you right now, but I believe that you could be of considerable use to us."

Jessica frowned.

"I would like to make you an offer."

An offer…

The utterance of the words caused Jessica's face to twist in anger. She knew a refusal of Sinclair's proposal would result in her death. And yet, the thought of even feigning interest in an attempt to obtain her freedom sickened her with a feeling of cheap cowardice. "Stick your offer up your ass!" She spat through angrily clenched teeth.

Looking away from Jessica, Sinclair exhaled with a frustrated sigh as he rose to his feet once more. Turning his back to her, he took several steps before stopping to stand still. "Your incorruptibility amazes me Detective," he finally said after a bout of silence, his back remaining to her as he spoke. "Even in the face of death you are defiant."

Jessica renewed her attempts to free herself.

"Your father I am sure would be very proud of you on this night." Sinclair continued, turning to face his struggling captive once more with a mocking smile on his face. "It is truly a pity that you share his stubbornness, and that I have to kill you, just as I did him."

Jessica's eyes widened in absolute horror, her struggles gradually coming to a halt. The shock of Sinclair's revelation brought about a feeling akin to being punched in the stomach, her heart racing as she began to shake uncontrollably. Her father's killer, an individual whom she had been searching for her entire career, was now right here in front of her. And she was helpless.

"No... NO!" Driven by pure emotion, Jessica began to thrash wildly, resuming her attempts to escape her bonds with renewed vigor. Seconds passed, a malevolent smile forming on Sinclair's

face with the passing time. "YOU SON OF A
BITCH! I'LL KILL YOU!"

Her rage reverberated throughout the shed's
interior before she finally succumbed to
exhaustion, the rattling of her chains ceasing. Tears
streamed down her face as she choked on her own
anguish.

"You, son of a, bitch..."

Looking to David Mitchell, Sinclair gave a nod of
his head. In response, a hypodermic needle was
withdrawn from a pocket by the crooked officer. "If
it is any consolation to you Detective," Sinclair
started. "Your passing will be quicker and easier
than that of your father's."

Jessica gazed at the needle with terrified eyes.

"You'll be found in your home." Sinclair
continued. "After a simple injection of air into your
bloodstream."

"You won't get away with this." Jessica sniffled,
the flame of courage and hope no longer burning in
her voice.

"Of course I will Detective. You will be
pronounced dead as a result of a stroke, just as
Robert Kane was."

Jessica blanched, her fearful eyes wide as Sinclair
continued.

"It is unfortunate that such would happen to you
at such a young age, however, it is entirely possible,
Detective. A coroner who works for me can take
care of any stray details."

Jessica began to sob quietly. Sinclair turned his
attention to David once more. "Make it quick."

With that, he and the rest turned to depart, soon
leaving Jessica's sight as they exited the shed.

David removed the needle's plastic cap as he
advanced, Jessica's sobs continuing as he knelt
down before her. With his right hand, he pressed

the side of her head down against the floor, holding it firmly in place to expose the side of her neck.

"A pity it has to be this way Jessica."

Suddenly, David was sent tumbling over backward, a cry of alarm escaping him as he was quickly placed onto his back, as if pulled from behind. The needle sailed from his grasp to be lost in the dark as he crashed onto the earth, the wind knocked out of him from the landing. From her prone position, Jessica's eyes widened as she now saw the ninja looming over David, his fist soon descending to render him unconscious.

In awestruck silence, Jessica watched her rescuer kneel before her. "Clayton?"

The ninja's actions halted. A moment of silence followed.

"We have to get out of here." he finally said.

Pulling a throwing blade from within the v neck jacket of his costume, he bent over Jessica's back side. Within seconds, she could feel the zip tie release her wrists as the strap was cut. She watched as the tie around her ankles was dealt with in a similar manner. A sigh of relief escaping her once freed. Returning his weapon to whence it came, the ninja stood. "How did you find me?" Jessica asked as she was helped to her feet.

"I'm afraid now is a poor time for storytelling."

Jessica claimed David's sidearm from his unconscious body. Swiftly drawing the pistol from its holster, she popped out the clip to check it.

Loaded.

Replacing the clip, she followed behind her enigmatic ally, aiming the gun downward in a suppressed position as they carefully crept toward the shed's exit, each placing their back to the left wall. Cautiously, the ninja peered outside.

A thunderous explosion suddenly rocked the still night, the ninja instinctively ducking back into the shed's interior as a bullet struck its wall. "Shit!" Jessica exclaimed as she too ducked down. Four more shots followed.

"I had a feeling this wouldn't be easy." the ninja said, seeming oddly composed considering the situation.

Jessica stood quickly, returning fire upon Sinclair and his men as they began taking cover amid the yard's automobiles. A scream of pain erupted from one of the men, a bullet piercing his shoulder after a trio of shots. "We can't stay here." Jessica said, ducking once more just in time to avoid another hail of bullets.

The ninja's eyes narrowed as he quickly scanned the area. "You have to get out of here to tell your colleagues." the ninja said. "I'll try to draw their fire so you can make a run for it. Use the gun for cover fire if you have to."

"I'm not gonna just leave you."

More gunfire came.

"Listen, I should be able to use the yard to my advantage. I can probably lose them in the dark easily enough if I can't take them."

"That's crazy! You can't just..."

Jessica was interrupted mid-sentence as the ninja dove from their cover. Maintaining a crouching position, he executed a pair of forward rolls over his right shoulder, safely reaching the cover provided by a nearby pickup truck as Jessica looked on in near amazement. "Unbelievable." she muttered while unleashing a barrage of gunfire.

Sinclair and his men took cover as the ninja bolted, his dark lithe form swiftly moving through the yard as he dashed around and between the automobiles. Following his lead, Jessica sprung from the shed, continuing to open fire as she ran on. Suddenly, she heard a series of sharp clicks, the sounds replacing the explosion and recoil that previously came with each pull of the trigger. Her heart sank as a horrible realization came to her. The gun was empty.

Oh God, no.

Jessica dove to the ground as Sinclair's men retaliated. Crawling on her hands and knees, she managed to reach several nearby mounds of scrap parts. For a brief moment, she pondered the ninja's whereabouts, as she had quickly lost sight of him while trying to survive the war zone that she was now in. Reluctantly placing thoughts of his safety aside in her fears for her own, she scrambled to her feet as she began to run for her life.

Sinclair and company emerged from their cover. "I want them dead." he declared, his nostrils flaring.

Chief Higgins turned to Patricia Collins. "Find Jessica, the rest of us will get that mental case in the costume."

忍

Jessica ran for what seemed like eternity. Sharp rocks and gravel bit into her feet through her cotton socks as they pounded the packed dirt. Finally succumbing to pain and exhaustion, she stumbled suddenly, landing hard on the ground. Her heart raced, beating like a tiny bird in her chest as she began to frantically crawl. Her situation reminded her of absurd slasher movies, where young women fleeing from some unstoppable killer inevitably panic and die.

Get Up. Get Up. GET UP!

Struggling to stand again, she managed to hobble along a few more feet before dropping again to one knee. Leaning against an old used tire, she began looking around. A gasp caught in her throat as she suddenly saw movement in the distance amid the scattered junk. The brightness of the moon allowed her to easily make out the feminine form that seemed to be searching the refuse, stopping frequently to scan the area while aiming a gun ahead of her.

Patricia.

Jessica resumed crawling, trying to stay low to avoid being seen. She didn't think she could out run Patricia in her condition. She needed to find cover, try to take Patricia by surprise and subdue her. She was keenly aware of her bright clothes, knowing full well that if she wasn't careful, her pursuer could easily spot the cheery blue and white of her tank and shorts. She needed a good hiding place. If Patricia saw her before she could strike, she was dead.

Keeping low, she moved about while searching for a place to conceal herself. Coming to several stacks of used tires that where piled head high, she positioned herself behind the wall of rubber, the smell of oil and asphalt from the treads thick in her nose.

From her hiding place she frantically looked about her for some form of weapon, her eyes finding nothing nearby that seemed like a suitable bludgeon. She soon heard Patricia's footsteps drawing near, cautious movements that made light, quick taps on the dirt.

Shit.

Jessica quickly pressed her back to the wall of tires. Listening intensely, she attempted to gage Patricia's distance from her as she inched her way to the edge of the stack. She forced her breathing to quiet ragged gasps, hoping for the best as she nervously waited.

NOW!

With catlike agility, Jessica hopped onto her right foot as Patricia stepped next to the tires. Her left leg shot out from her side, coming around the edge of her concealment as she executed a hook kick. The heel of her foot caught a surprised Patricia in the mouth, loosening teeth as she staggered backwards from the impact of the blow.

Quickly moving to press her newly gained advantage, Jessica charged in. Slamming hard into Patricia, she seized her at the wrist in an attempt to wrest the pistol from her grasp, both crashing onto the hood of a rusted out white Buick sedan that sat nearby.

Maintaining her grip, Jessica climbed a straddle of Patricia, repeatedly bashing her hand against the surface of the car's hood, with the fourth slam finally relieving her of the weapon. Jessica's face suddenly contorted in agony as she felt Patricia's fingers within the lengthy strands of her hair. Pain shot through her scalp as Patricia pulled her aside, rolling over to land on top of her as she tumbled off of the car's hood and onto the ground.

Fingers wrapped tightly around Jessica's throat, her face grimacing as Patricia began to squeeze. Instinctively, she grabbed Patricia's wrists, fighting to pull her hands away from her throat. Kicking and squirming beneath Patricia's weight, her movements soon grew more sluggish with each passing second. Her consciousness was quickly fading.

Jessica desperately grappled at Patricia's form in a last ditch effort to push her away. Grabbing Patricia's belt, she felt a small pouch, its composition comprised of familiar hard leather. Unsnapping a button cover at its top, she dug for the pouch's contents, the feeling of cool steel in her grasp as a metallic clacking sound accompanied the item's extraction.

Handcuffs.

With her fingers wrapped firmly around her new-found weapon, Jessica bashed the handcuffs against the side of Patricia's head, her grip loosening from around Jessica's throat as the blow caught her in the jaw just beneath the ear. Jessica swung the handcuffs again, with the second blow landing near Patricia's temple, rendering her unconscious as she fell to the ground.

Jessica struggled to her feet. Leaning against the side of the Buick, she gasped for air as she began to enjoy her returned ability to breathe. Seconds passed as her strength slowly began to return.

The sound of gunshots from elsewhere in the junkyard caused Jessica to jerk up in alarm. She knew that Sinclair and his men were firing at the ninja. She knew beneath the black clad form that seemed at times to be almost superhuman, was a man, a man with enormous courage and compassion, a man who was now laying his life on the line to ensure her survival, for the second time.

Jessica could easily escape the junkyard. She could now go to others on the police force, and with the evidence she now had. She could bring Rolland Sinclair, The Medicine Man, her father's killer to justice. She knew that without the ninja's aid however, none of this would be possible. She owed him so much, and despite the dangers of going back, she knew what she had to do, what was the right thing to do.

I can't leave him.

Jessica quickly set about handcuffing Patricia's wrists behind her. Standing again, she glanced around the front of the Buick, soon spotting Patricia's pistol as it remained where it had fell from the earlier struggle. Quickly claiming the gun, she began limping back into the junkyard.

"KILL HIM!"

Sinclair's commands were drowned out by a continual barrage of gunfire. Round after round shattered the windows of the cars as the black clad figure dashed on, his form disappearing amid the cover provided by the stationary vehicles and showers of exploding glass.

All was still again as Sinclair's men scanned the area, the seconds of silence dragging in the dark.

"Where the hell did he go?" Chief Higgins asked to no one in particular, the quiet night giving no reply.

"Spread out and find him." Sinclair said, his voice commanding even as he inched closer to Chief Higgins, as he himself was unarmed.

The men began to fan out. Cautiously they checked around the cars, their guns held out in front of them as they widened their search. Tension mounted with each silent second that passed. All remained still.

Suddenly in a flash of movement, a dark silhouette that darted between abandoned vehicles only to disappear an instant later. With each glimpse of the target, one of Sinclair's men would fire desperately at the point where the figure had disappeared into the darkness, the figure seeming unharmed as this scenario would play out again for another man, with even Chief Higgins seeming unable to score a hit.

"The son of a bitch is toying with us." Chief Higgins said, a tiny tinge of fear resonating in his voice.

"He's just a man." Sinclair reminded resolutely.

The hunt continued, with Sinclair's men soon separated from each other by several yards. The ninja emerged from behind one of the men, a tall, slim man in a green coat. The Ninja's right hand swiftly intercepted the man's arm as he turned to aim his pistol. Forcefully, he pushed the palm of his left hand into the extended arm at the elbow. The man cried out in pain at the elbow's hyper-extension, the pistol leaving his grasp as the Ninja pivoted to spin him around by the arm. In a flash, the man smashed face first through the back window glass of nearby automobile, his form from the waist down left to hang comically out of the back portion of the car's cab, the Ninja vanishing from the scene before others could investigate the disturbance.

Darting out from the cover of an old gray van, the Ninja flanked another of his pursuers. Before the man could turn to face him, the ninja quickly flung his arm out, the clattering of metal links following his limbs full extension. The business end of a weighted fighting chain sailed smoothly through the air, smacking smartly into the man's jaw. Enamel flew from his mouth as the surprisingly small, but heavy weight hit him squarely, sending him to the ground. The ninja was gone again while his cry of pain still hung in the air.

From elsewhere in the junkyard, Chief Higgins swallowed hard, holding his revolver before him, as another cry of pain from one of their own erupted in the dark.

"He's picking us off." Sinclair murmured a tone of awe and dread mixed into his voice.

Suddenly, Chief Higgins and Sinclair where sent tumbling to the ground, the dark figure of the ninja sending them sprawling to their faces as he struck from behind. Sinclair was immediately seized, strong hands held the lapels of his jacket, gasping as he was dragged roughly to his feet. Angry eyes glared into his as he was finally face to face with the ninja.

Chief Higgins quickly pushed himself up to one knee, turning simultaneously to aim his gun. Before he could fire, the ninja pivoted to face him, pushing Sinclair around in front of him to act as a shield. The heel of a foot planted firmly into Sinclair's mid-section sent him tumbling roughly back into Higgins, knocking them both to the ground again as Sinclair landed on top of the Chief.

The ninja turned his attention from the pair as the last of Sinclair's men suddenly emerged from amid the vehicles. Quickly the ninja crouched down, two shots from the man's gun passing harmlessly over him as he executed a forward roll over his left shoulder. Coming to his feet, he let his right arm fan outward towards him. A thick, billowing cloud formed in the air as a gritty blinding powder flew from his open hand.

Instinctively, the man threw his arms up to shield his eyes. The ninja rolled again, bringing himself close enough to strike the momentarily blinded man as he sprung to his feet.

Chief Higgins and Sinclair scrambled to their feet, Sinclair ducking behind the veteran police officer once again. Higgins readied his pistol again, watching from behind the gun's sights for the right moment to send a bullet into the conflict, the peppery dust still hanging lightly in the air as he tried to take aim.

The ninja lunged forward. His left leg in the lead, his left arm swung outward to successfully knock the gun arm aside as the man again attempted to fire. Taking a step forward, the ninja brought his right arm up, his hand forming onto an angular, roof like shape before its edge slammed hard into the man's exposed neck. The man's gun fell from his grasp as the blow sent him sprawling backwards onto the packed earth, his hand favoring his neck as his face contorted in agony.

The thunderclap sound of a gunshot going off nearby blasted the ninja's ears. Swiftly he spun in response, looking behind him where the noise still rung in the air. Kneeling several yards away was Jessica, a smoking pistol in her hands pointing straight ahead of her, held steady despite the ragged breaths coming from her chest.

Chief Higgins lay flat on his back in the dirt. Blood from a lethal bullet wound poured and spread from his white crested chest. He wasn't moving.

Jessica turned the gun on Sinclair, her teeth clenched tight as she glared at her target with malice filled eyes. Sinclair's eyes widened in terror.

"No Jessica." The ninja said, his voice steady and soothing. "Don't do this."

Tears streamed freely down Jessica's cheeks. Her index finger tensed against the pistol's trigger. Her hands began to tremble.

"Vengeance only stains you." the ninja said, continuing his attempts at reason. "Killing him won't bring your father back."

With unsteady legs, Jessica slowly rose to her feet. For a brief moment, her mind traveled back to her father's last moments. His kindly voice echoed in her mind, trying to instill the moral fortitude that he wanted her to have even in death's coming.

'Don't confuse Justice with revenge Jessica. Justice is about balance and harmony. It's what you as a police officer, should strive for.'

She continued to glare at Sinclair from behind the pistol. Wailing police sirens became audible in the distance.

"On your stomach, Mr. Sinclair." she finally commanded. "Arms spread. Now."

Slowly, Sinclair lowered himself to the ground, the volume of the sirens growing louder.

Jessica turned her attention to the ninja. "You should get out of..."

The ninja was gone.

Chapter 16

Medicine Man Brought To Justice, Extreme Police Corruption Exposed By Incorruptible Police Hero.

By Clayton Drake

Elmira NY- In a shocking turn of events, local philanthropist Roland Sinclair has been revealed to be the drug lord known as the Medicine Man. In the aftermath of a shootout that took place in the Elmira Salvage Yard late in the night, Detective Jessica Devins, of the Elmira Police Department managed to overcome impossible odds, subduing the drug lord along with five of his men. Police Chief William Higgins along with officers David Mitchell and Patricia Collins were also at the scene and revealed to be working with Sinclair. In addition to other charges, Mitchell and Collins are being charged with abduction after reportedly taking Detective Devins from her home by force. Higgins lost his life after a fatal wound sustained during the shoot-out. Paramedics declared him dead at the scene.

"They wanted me to join them." Detective Jessica Devins later commented. "I swore an oath, and the thought of an officer breaking that oath in a way such as that sickens me. I would never involve myself in something like that, and I can only hope that such acts have done nothing to damage the people's trust in this fine department." When asked how she had managed to overcome such adversity, Detective Devins said "I guess someone was watching out for me. I was very lucky." Most of Sinclair's men claimed to have been attacked by another who aided Detective Devins. No evidence of such was found at the scene, nor were any further comments given to support this by the Elmira Police Department.

忍

Seated at his desk, Clayton Drake admired his work. He read it to himself with a keen eye for errors, his lips forming into a smile as he stared at the monitor before him.

Just in time for today's edition.

With his story completed, he stood from his desk. He reached for his keys nearby, suddenly pausing mid-movement. Holding this position, his eyes turned briefly toward his shoulder, the sleeve of his gray t-shirt having shifted up slightly at his arm's extension to reveal hints of medical treatment.

Claiming his keys, he turned to leave. Stopping briefly, he returned his gaze to the shoulder, lifting his sleeve to reveal a white gauze pad, held to his shoulder by strips of medical tape. He sighed, remembering how he had gotten the wound, how a bullet in the salvage yard managed to graze his arm.

Close call.

Pulling the sleeve back down to cover his bandages, he continued on, deftly making his way through the busy offices around him and out the doors of the *Elmira Star*, the glass entrance stenciled with the logo for the paper. Looking around while making his way across the spacious parking lot outside the brown industrial brick building, he stopped next to the white 2005 Pontiac Grand Prix that was his car.

He watched the activity of the city for a brief moment. Kids walked down the nearby sidewalk, laughing and joking amongst themselves. A city bus rumbled past as a young couple happily walked a dog towards the small riverside park. He grinned as he thought of the city. Free of the Medicine Man's corruption. Elmira was a bit brighter, a bit better place to live. Justice had prevailed. The ninja had prevailed.

Still smiling, Clayton entered his vehicle and drove off, the car merging with the city's traffic just as the ninja would merge with the shadows. The invisible warrior, seen by none.

The pounding of the gavel was the sweetest sound Jessica had heard in a long time, as it signaled the resolution of four grueling months at trial. The end had finally come for the Medicine Man, as Roland Sinclair now faced life in prison for his crimes, the murder of Jessica's father included. A weak smile crossed her face as she filed out with the crowd of people that left the courtroom.

Epilogue

A gentle breeze whisked through the stillness of the cemetery. Dried leaves of red and gold rustled along the grass, tumbling over and around the feet of Detective Jessica Devins. Strands of her lengthy red hair trailed through the cool autumn air as she stood in somber silence, her gaze cast down to the face of the stone marker erected before her.

IN LOVING MEMORY OF
ROBERT DEVINS
Loving Husband and Father
Forever missed

"He'd be proud of you."
Jessica spun around at the sound of a soft familiar voice.
"Clayton."
With a brown leather bomber jacket slung casually over his shoulder he approached her, his cat like tread almost silent and devoid of sloppy motor skills. Jessica turned back to her father's stone as he came up beside her. He placed his free hand on her shoulder, his touch gentle and comforting.

"You ok?" he asked softly.

"Yeah, I'm okay..."

"I'm sorry." Clayton said, offering condolence as he too gazed at the monument.

"Thank you." Jessica said, her voice quaking slightly. "You have my sympathy for your loss too."

Clayton managed a weak smile, turning his attention back to Jessica as she looked up at him.

"I never got to say thank you," she continued, her voice breaking slightly as ushered tears shined in her eyes. "For everything you did for me."

"You don't have to thank me, nor do you owe me anything."

"No Clayton..." she said, stopping him with an upturned hand. "I owe you everything. I couldn't have done this without you. If it wasn't for you, I would have..." Her voice died away as the tears finally fell down her cheeks.

"We helped each other Jessica. You stopped me from being shot in the back. You saved my life."

Jessica smiled in spite of herself, wiping a tear away as Clayton continued.

"We accomplished what neither one of us could have done alone. We did this together."

Jessica turned her gaze to her feet. An air of almost child-like innocence hung about her, despite the shame that was in her voice as she continued.

"Sinclair took loved ones from both of us. Only you had what it took to do what was right."

"Jessica..." Clayton started.

"I wanted to kill him, Clayton." she interrupted, looking up at him once more as she shook her head, fresh tears blooming. "I was gonna kill him..."

"But you didn't. In the end, you did what was right. Truth be told, I think you would have even if I hadn't been there. You're very strong."

"I'm tired of being strong." she whispered.

Gently, Clayton pulled Jessica to him, wrapping an arm around her in a sympathetic embrace. "Hey, it's okay..."

She buried her face into his chest. Emotion welled up from inside her, coming to the surface easily with this simple act of compassion. He felt warm against her cool face as she soon wrapped her arms around him, silent sobs shaking her.

Minutes passed as she slowly began to quiet, his comfort blanketing her. The pleasant smell of his leather coat and strong soap tickled her nose. She breathed deeply and contentedly.

"The authorities are still looking for you." she finally said, her voice steady again. "What are you gonna do?"

"Would it be safe to assume you haven't shared the knowledge of my identity with them?"

A slight chuckle crept from Jessica's mouth as she looked up at him gently, finally pushing her face away from the warmth of his chest.

"Yeah,it would. Your secret is safe."

"Then I'll endure..." Clayton said while casually brushing an errant strand of hair from Jessica's face with his index finger. "And I'll move on with my life."

Jessica only stared, pondering his words as he continued. "Tragedy and sorrow are as much a part of life as joy. We can't stop seeing the world with eyes that love, despite those like Sinclair who do not. We will honor our loved ones, and hold them in our hearts."

A brief silence hung in the air as each looked into the eyes of the other. Clayton finally grinned softly, his hand reaching up to gently brush Jessica's cheek. "If you ever need me, I'll be there for you." Jessica took Clayton's hand. Turning the palm up, she placed something in it. "This belongs to you."

Clayton could feel the caress of cool steel in his palm. Casting his gaze down, he saw the metal four pointed star that he had lost many nights before. "My shuriken..." he smiled. "Thank you Jessica." With that he slowly turned to leave.

For a moment Jessica watched him depart, her hand unconsciously rising to touch against her cheek for a moment. "Clayton?" she finally called out.

He stopped and turned, his eyes wondering. "Yes?"

Jessica took a few quick steps towards him until catching up to him once more. "I... I'm not much of a cook, but I... ummm, thought about having spaghetti tonight. Would you like to come over for dinner?"

Clayton grinned, his head nodding slightly in acceptance of the invitation. "That sounds nice. I'd like that."

Side by side, they made their way along the paved pathway. As they proceeded through the cemetery gates, Jessica took Clayton's hand into her own.

About Author

Trace Richards resides in the wilds between the small towns of Clarksville and Louisiana, Missouri. A practitioner of martial arts, he lives in isolation with only his wife and many pets. He will continue his ambitions in ways of both pen and sword as he works on his next book. This is his first book.

Shadow
Of
Perseverance

The sun shined brightly from a clear sky above as the evening traffic flowed freely along the road known to area residents as Baldwin Street. Vehicles of various sizes, makes, and models carried their drivers to and from destinations as they went about their private endeavors. Easily blending with the scene was a white Pontiac Grand Prix. The brown eyes of the car's driver gazed at the road ahead, each of the man's hands grasping the steering wheel at its sides.

Strands of his short brown hair were whipped about by the air that rushed in through the car's open windows. Flicking his left hand upward, he activated the car's right turn signal, alerting other drivers to his intended direction of travel before turning into the parking lot of a large building of tan brick. Cruising amid the parked cars, he stopped the car in a vacant space before the building, the words *Elmira Star* spelled across the upper front of the structure in bold brown letters.

Vacating his vehicle, the man stopped momentarily. He cast his gaze skyward, the dark green t-shirt and blue jeans that he wore slightly strained by his slender yet sinewy frame. Hints of a grin began to show as a pair of starlings flew overhead.

Returning his gaze to his destination, the man continued on. The soles of his tan hiking boots making nary a sound upon the pavement as he strode across the parking lot. A gentle shove sent glass doors to swing inward as he passed beneath the blue roof of a glass awning.

Walls of white encased the news paper's offices as he entered. Warm smiles and greetings met him at nearly every turn as he made his way through the hustle and bustle of the ending workday that carried on around him. Stopping at a desk with a computer atop it, he pulled open one of its drawers. A gruff voice suddenly called out behind him as he casually rummaged through the drawer's contents.

"Back already Mr. Drake?"

Closing the desk drawer, Clayton Drake turned. Standing before him was an older man of plump stature, clad in a plain brown suit with a white dress shirt and black tie. The buttons of his shirt seemed strained by the roundness of his belly as he stood with his hands in the pockets of his pants. A thick gray mustache partially hid his upper lip, a severe contrast to the balding gray atop his head.

Clayton smiled at the paper's publisher while holding up a pair of dark glasses in his right hand.

"Just came back for these..."

The publisher grinned, a good humored chuckle seeping out of him as Clayton donned the sun glasses before departing once more.

"See you tomorrow morning sir..."

Randy Kent...

Sadness clutched at Clayton's heart as he stared at the name inscribed on the headstone. He still couldn't believe that his nephew was gone, having lost his life at just fourteen years of age. It had been nearly a year since the funeral, his death the result of a drug overdose.

Standing quietly, Clayton turned his eyes to a man and woman who stood together at his side. Both were garbed casually, the dark haired man watching quietly as the woman knelt over the grave to place a bundle of flowers over it. Standing once more, Martha Kent took her husband's hand into her own. "I still miss him so much, Paul." she said, stifling tears as she and her husband embraced.

"I miss him too Martha." Clayton said while turning his eyes back to the grave. "Even in my own grief, I can't begin to imagine yours. The most painful thing a parent can do is lose a child."

A few seconds passed as all three stared at their shared loss in silence. "You have work tonight." Martha finally said to her husband. With Paul's arm around her, she and her husband turned to depart. "Thank you for coming." Paul said as he turned to Clayton.

"Of course." he replied. "Call me if you need anything at all."

"Take care of yourself Clayton." Martha said.

Clayton watched as Martha and Paul made their way down the paved pathway leading toward the gates of Woodlawn Cemetery. A slight grin began to form as he reflected briefly on he and Martha's relationship. Seven years separated he and his older sibling, and at the age of forty-two, she'd changed very little. She still enjoyed peace and quiet, content to simply sit down and enjoy good book as she did on many nights. He was in many ways her polar opposite; spontaneous, creative, and always looking for an adventure or journey of some sort. Perhaps it was those very traits that took him down his given path in life.

Turning his gaze back on the headstone of Randy's burial place, his smile faded. His path in life had taken a darker turn, and he knew he would have to tread carefully, least he fall into an abyss of misery and rage from which he would never come back from. With a final, silent vow to a deceased loved one, he turned and prepared to embark on yet another journey; one to pursue and bring justice. It was one that he was prepared, and had been preparing to make, for some time.

忍

The white Grand Prix slowed to a stop at the end of the gravel driveway. The soft chirping of birds could be heard all around as Clayton vacated his car. The rustling of leaves caressed his ears as a gentle breeze sent the limbs of nearby trees to sway.

With a folded up newspaper, and a small black box in hand, Clayton began making his way toward his simple country home. The white, single story house was surrounded by an air of quaintness. The serene jingle of a wind chime rang in the air as a seated swing hung silently from the overhang of the front porch.

Claiming a handful of envelopes from a mailbox at the base of the porch's steps, Clayton made his way up to the front door; unlocking it with a key before stepping inside. Light poured in from a kitchen window as he made his way through the dwelling's living room to stop before an island in the center of its adjacent kitchen. Setting the newspaper and box onto the counter top's surface, he began sorting through the collection of envelopes which formed the bulk of his mail for the day. Pausing, he lay all but one aside, his mouth forming a grin as he saw that it was a letter from Japan.

Mindful of the envelope's contents, Clayton tore the top open and extracted the sheet of paper that was inside. Unfolding the letter, he scanned over the rows of Japanese calligraphy, each character seeming like a work of art. Clayton's grin transformed into a smile as he easily translated the letter to himself.

Dear Clayton,
It is my hopes that this letter finds you in bountiful health and spirit. In all my years, few of the gifts that life has saw fit to bestow upon me have brought more joy than having you as my pupil. I was fearful of your intentions when you first declared your desire to return to your homeland, as I too felt the anger and sadness that accompanied the loss of your beloved nephew. In your time as my student, I always did my utmost to teach you that the blade that gives and preserves life will always be stronger than the one that takes it. It is my hope that you will continue to hold true to the ways of budo in the pursuit of justice I know you soon plan to embark on. Never stray from the path and hold to always the Precepts of Perseverance in the Martial Ways; principles of guidance that have been handed down by those before us.

Remember always that what ever hardship you may endure is but temporary.
Always behave correctly.

*Remember that hate and sorrow are both part of life;
understand that they too are gifts from the gods.*
Never fall prey to egoism, or avarice.
*Never stray from the path of the spirit or that of the
martial arts; always seek ambition in ways of both the
pen and the sword.*

*I look forward to hearing from you again soon, and
dearly hope that our paths will again cross one day.*
Love and happiness always,
Tomoharu Yoshida

Clayton's grin widened as his thoughts
returned to times past. He well remembered the
twists and turns of his life, and how it was that
he came to meet Tomoharu; a man who would
forever alter that life.

Born and raised in Elmira New York, Clayton
Drake had lived in the city of over thirty
thousand for most of his life. Coming from a
small family, his older sister Martha was his only
sibling. A student of Elmira Free Academy, he
excelled in language arts and sports, particularly
track and field. After his high school graduation,
his education would continue at Elmira College;
where he would graduate with a major in English
Literature. A pursued interest in photography
would also earn him an Art minor.

Soon after completion of college, Clayton
would find work as a photojournalist for the
famed monthly publication known as *National
Geographic Magazine.* It was during this time that
he would see much of the world in his career, and
eventually journey to Japan for his first time
while on an assignment to do an article on the
origin of Japan's shadowy warriors known as the
ninja. After an exhaustive search, Clayton's quest

for answers would eventually lead him to a quaint tea house, and a meeting with Tomoharu. He had finally found what he was looking for, as Tomoharu was a distant descendent of Hattori Hanzo, the legendary ninja who served as protection for the shogun responsible for the eventual unification of Japan and the end of its feudal era; Ieyasu Tokugawa.

In the course of several interviews, Clayton gleaned much from Tomoharu, and was able to finish his feature article on Japan's ninja upon his return to the United States. His interest and desire to learn had grown beyond that which was required to write a simple piece for a magazine however, and two years later he would return to Japan in hopes that Tomoharu would teach him the ways of Ninjutsu; the art of invisibility.

"Only one with a benevolent heart and sincere intentions should pursue Ninjutsu..." Tomoharu told him. He stared at Clayton for several seconds, as though he were studying him before continuing. "Ninja as we have discussed before are not the shadowy assassins of your movies in America. They are persons of endurance and perseverance. The skills of the ninja are not to be for entertainment or personal gain. Do you understand?" Clayton nodded.

"I understand sir."

Sensing Clayton's sincerity, the elderly man's mouth shaped into a grin and Clayton's training in the way of stealth would thus begin. In the course of this apprenticeship, the man he would come to call Sensei would constantly stress three guiding principles.

To hide is defense...
Violence is to be avoided...
Use of the sword is for peace, and to protect family, country, and nature...

The next decade would see Clayton train rigorously in the ninja's combat and espionage arts. Empty hand fighting technique that employed use of the entire body was just the beginning. Known as Taijutsu, the strikes, grappling, and ground hitting rolls of the method were repeated to perfection, often times on frozen ponds and other slippery or uneven surfaces to train in balance.

Use of the ninja's assorted weapons and tools were also mastered. He learned to wield staves of varying lengths, Japanese style swords and pole-arms, *Shuriken* throwing blades, and even stranger combat tools such as the *Kusari Gama* chain and sickle and the *Shuko* clawed bands.

Clayton attained the mastery of stealth for which the ninja were legendary. With agility and patience, he could tread silently on any surface, and utilize his surroundings to conceal his form and intentions through various methods of disguise and camouflage.

Through spiritual methods rooted in Tibetan and Chinese traditions, Clayton also learned meditation skills which utilized breathing, visualization, and internalization. It was through this training that he would achieve a rare skill; the ability to sense an attack or feel the intent of another to do harm.

"There are situations where one may not even realize that they have an adversary." Tomoharu once said to him. "In some instances, you may not even have a chance to react to an attacker. You must trust what you feel and train to hone your senses to a sensitivity beyond that of most. It is with this sensitivity that you can receive input beyond your physical senses, what some would call premonitions of danger..."

Legends of the ninja were rich with tales of how they could accomplish a myriad of seemingly supernatural feats. Despite all that Clayton had experienced in the course of his apprenticeship, he met the notion of any mystical or psychic power with skepticism. Yet it was something that Tomoharu spoke of with utmost sincerity. "Allow me to show you..."

The elderly man placed a sword in Clayton's hand. Turning his back to Clayton, he gently lowered himself to his knees with his hips resting upon his heels. His back was straight as his gaze leveled ahead. He looked at ease as his hands rested atop his thighs and his eyes closed. A look of confusion stretched across Clayton's face as he stared down at his sensei.

"An impulse of thought always accompanies an action of violence." Tomoharu said. "People, and animals too, give off this impulse. This is known as the force of the killer, or *Sakki,* and it can be perceived by one who is sensitive enough to do so..."

In almost disbelief in what Tomoharu was suggesting, Clayton could only stare at the sword, a blade that he had become very familiar with in the course of his training. The long curved *saya* scabbard of black lacquered wood stretched from one hand to the other. Clayton knew that the slightly curved and razor sharp blade housed inside was much shorter, to deceive an opponent into thinking the blade would take longer to draw as well as to facilitate combat in tighter spaces. In ancient times, the extra space in the scabbard's bottom would also be used to hide blinding powders or other things. The *tsuba* hand guard at the blade's base was little more than a oval of black hammered steel, as it lacked the glamor or ornate work that was typical of the samurai's longer *katana* sword. "I am waiting..." Tomoharu said, snapping Clayton out of his thoughts.

Slowly, Clayton raised the sword above his head. Seconds passed. "Your intentions to harm me must be true." Tomoharu declared in the face of Clayton's hesitancy. "The sakki will not be there to detect otherwise..."

"This is madness Sensei..."

Only silence followed the protest, as the old man waited. Clayton's eyes squeezed shut. His teeth clenched, the mere thought of harming one who had given him so much seeming unbearable. Still, Tomoharu remained seated. Finally managing to muster the inner resolve needed to carry out the deed, Clayton brought the blade downward.

In a flash, the old man rolled to his right; the sword slicing only air as is passed through the space he had occupied seconds before. Clayton could only stare in astonishment as he could see no way that Tomoharu could have known when the attack was coming. The old man held a crouching position as he grinned at Clayton.

In the years to pass, Clayton's training continued in the formidable combat and stealth methods. Tomoharu would occasionally test him for the seemingly psychic ability to sense an incoming attack. Many a time he would kneel with his sensei standing at his back, a wooden stick held to strike. Time and again the stick would strike his flesh and bones, the bruises left an indication of another failed attempt to sense the teacher's intentions.

On one fateful afternoon, Clayton was seated at tea with his mentor. The old man suddenly stood from his seat upon the wooden floor, leaving Clayton to sup alone. Seconds passed as Clayton waited for the elderly man's return, the passing time causing him to ponder the abrupt departure. As he raised the small tea cup to his mouth once more, a sudden sense of dread began to tug at him. The ominous feeling was something he had never experienced before and was at a loss to explain. He knew but one thing with absolute certainty. He needed to move.

Clayton dove and rolled to his left. A sharp crack blasted his ears as he spun to see a slender wooden pole strike the floor. His eyes followed the stick's length to find Tomoharu grasping it at the end. The old man smiled. "Very good." he said. Clayton could only stare up at his mentor as he realized he had passed the test. He had felt the force of the killer.

A month later, tragedy struck as he received a news from his homeland of America; a letter from his sister which bared news of the death of her son, his young nephew, Randy. Anger welled inside him as learned that the teenaged boy had died from a massive drug overdose.

Determined to find the one responsible, Clayton made preparations to return to America. An online search and email correspondences landed him a home in the Elmira area, and an impressive resume earned him a job as a writer for the city's local newspaper. Disassembled weaponry, armor, and ninja tools were sent ahead of him through overseas shipping methods to arrive at his new home, where he would reassemble them himself.

After the funeral, he spent much of the year to follow modifying his house in the same manner as those of the feudal era ninja had done. He built false floor boards and concealed doorways into the dwelling to hide gear and facilitate escape should such became necessary. Everything was soon ready, and he could begin his investigations.

Clayton's thoughts returned to the current moment. Setting the letter aside, he turned his attention to the newspaper before him, taking a brief moment to read the bold headline of the front page's cover story.

Detective Encourages Kids to 'Just Say No'
by Clayton Drake
Below the headline was a photograph of a woman with long red hair. A wall of tan brick served as a background as her lips held a warm grin for the photographer. Visible from the hips up, her hands were clasped behind her in a relaxed manner as lengthy strands of her hair flowed over the shoulders of a plain dark blue turtle neck style sweater that she wore.

Clayton knew the article well. He had written the piece just two days ago, covering a Detective Jessica Devins, and her involvement in a drug free program at Parley Coburn Elementary School that week. His smile fading, he opened the black box and scanned over various cosmetics that were inside. With the makeup kit in hand, he turned from the island to begin preparations for the night's search.

Detective Jessica Devins breathed a deep sigh as she scanned the classroom. A sea of young eyes stared back at her from the floor below, the number of boys and girls seated before her numbering near thirty. At her left side stood a young raven haired woman. Clad in a bright red blouse, a white ankle length skirt, and black leather flats, she clapped her hands together four times to gain the attention of the students before her.

"OK everyone," the teacher said. "I'd like for you all to thank Detective Devins for taking the time to come in and speak with you this week."

"Thank you, Detective Devins." the class said in unison. Jessica only smiled to her young audience. "Everyone have a great weekend." the teacher said, bringing the day to end. En mass, the students left their seats, the sigh of relief that escaped Jessica lost amid the sea of children who were eager to get out of school.

忍

A gentle breeze whisked through the air as Jessica strode out through the double glass doors of the school. Amid the children preparing to make their way home, she paused at the base of the concrete steps that lead to the long, two story building of tan brick. Looking back, her gaze traveled up the Grecian-style pillars that rose from beside the school's entrance. The windows lining the buildings front almost seemed to stare blankly back at her, a warm grin forming as she reflected back on her time with the children.

It had been an awkward week for Jessica. Working with children and giving presentations had been somewhat outside of her comfort zone. Still, it was her hope that her efforts had touched their lives in some small way. Perhaps her lectures and cautions regarding the dangers of drug use would serve to send them down a path in life that was free of substance abuse, and the ruin she had seen it bring to so many. In spite of her anxieties, she felt a twinge of sadness to see her time with the students end.

Turning away from the school once more, Jessica's smile faded. With a final silent farewell, she walked down the concrete walkway;

returning to her pursuit and apprehension of those who flooded the streets with the very poisons that she had warned the students about.

Street lights glowed boldly against the night's darkness as Clayton strolled silently amid passersby on the sidewalk, easily blending with the hustle and bustle on Church Street. The application of cosmetics had darkened the complexion of his skin, giving him a more downtrodden and grimy appearance. A pair of tattered black pants, a gray shirt, and a worn brown coat with a black stocking cap completed his disguise, garments he had easily acquired from the local Good Will. Continuing on, he decided to investigate a seedy part of the area around a nearby short line bus station.

As good a place as any to start...

The hum of the dryer and the tumbling of the clothing within it reverberated throughout the red brick of the basement's walls. Clad in a simple blue t-shirt and a pair of black cotton trousers with elastic around the waist and ankles, Jessica glided across a large mat of green foam that covered a portion of the concrete the floor. The tails of a golden silk sash that was tied around her waist trailed with her seamless movements as she wielded a pair of short single edged swords with broad blades and hand guards. Her hair whipped through the air while tied in a simple ponytail as she twirled about in an elegant dance; executing a combination of simulated thrusts, slashes, and kicks.

Shuffling forward with her left foot in the lead, Jessica executed an upward slash with her left palm out before rotating the arm to execute a downward one. Withdrawing her left arm as she stepped forward, she repeated the simulated attacks with her right arm before lashing out with a front kick from her left leg. Turning quickly to face her rear, she unleashed a sudden flurry of alternating left and right thrusts before stepping back into a defensive stance again.

With her left arm held up over her head in preparation to deliver another attack, she extended her right arm horizontally as the blades of both swords pointed straight ahead. Pausing in this position, she gazed forward with determined eyes as a sudden realization befell her. The dryer had stopped. Her laundry was done.

With a sigh of fatigue, Jessica's arms lowered as she relaxed her guard. Strolling to the washing machine, she placed the butterfly swords within a small plastic laundry basket which sat atop it. Her lips shaped into a slight grin as the remembered how she had come to be trained in the Chinese martial art of Wing Chun Kung Fu, and how a chance encounter with a Chinese immigrant who lived just four houses down from her would come about as she rode her bicycle one summer day.

Seeing the young man wielding the very swords that she now possessed, she stopped and watched him in his yard as her curiosity peaked. Although he moved away with his wife after just three years, she had learned a great deal during her time spent in training, and he had allowed her to keep the butterfly swords in honor of the bond he had formed with her and her family.

Her thoughts returning from the past, Jessica opened the dryer. Removing an assortment of now clean and dry garments, she tossed them into the basket as well before making her way back upstairs.

The tan carpet's fibers caressed the soles of her feet through clean black socks as she placed the laundry basket on the far end of her sofa before taking a seat next to it. As she began setting about the task of sorting and folding, the sound of a news broadcast on the television across the room snagged her attention. Stopping in the middle of folding a dark blue sweatshirt, her eyes narrowed as she listened to the raven haired woman in a brown sports jacket that was on screen.

"In other news, police investigations into the drug lord authorities are calling The Medicine Man are nearing their fifth year. Elmira Police Chief William Higgins has refused to comment at this time regarding..."

The remote to the TV landed onto the coffee table with a rough clatter, Jessica having discarded it after turning off the television in frustration. With an exasperated sigh, she leaned back in her seat; the shirt that she had yet to begin folding still in her lap. Soon becoming lost in thought once more, her gaze fell to rest on the table, and the handcuffs and badge that lay inert upon it

"C'mon dude, pass it over!"

Expectorating violently, the youth handed the joint over to his friend after having taken a long drag from it. "Man, that's potent stuff." he coughed.

"Dude, this ain't shit." the other replied while taking a drag himself as his lack of a cough suggested more experience with smoking marijuana. "You wanna get some really good shit?"

"Sure..."

Finishing the joint, the youth flicked the remainder into an open dumpster; paying no mind to the dirty vagrant who lay curled up nearby in a pile of trash in the dark alleyway.

"I know this place on Southside. I got a hundred bucks. C'mon..."

Emerging from the alleyway, the two teenage boys set out to get their next fix as Clayton sat up from the trash pile.

Hmmm... I guess the third time is a charm.

Three straight nights of reconnaissance had finally paid off. He had found a lead to the Elmira drug trade. His blood ran cold at the thought of the two boys taking the same poisons that had claimed the life of his nephew. Yet to interfere with their intentions would cut his only chance to find those that were responsible.

Emerging from behind the alley, he merged with the passersby along the sidewalk. Maintaining a safe distance from the boys so as not to be spotted while tailing them, he pondered how best to accomplish his goals as well as save their lives.

Perhaps the police can be utilized to serve that end...

Steam erupted from the white ceramic mug as Jessica filled it with coffee.

"Another night in paradise, eh Detective?" a jovial voice said as a plump black man in police uniform joined her side. "Oh yeah." Jessica replied with a sarcastic smirk. "Love it here so much I don't think I'll ever leave."

Officer Walter Briggs chuckled as Jessica offered to fill his own mug.

"Much obliged. How goes the search for the elusive Medicine Man?"

Jessica turned her eyes to him in an annoyed manner.

"The case has been on-going for close to five years now Walter. You really have to ask?"

Jessica took a sip of her coffee. "Well, in your defense Detective, you've only been on the case for the past couple of years." Walter said. "Year and a half," Jessica corrected with a sarcastic smirk. "Please don't make my failure any more monumental than it already is."

"Keep that chin up, Detective." Walter said reassuringly. "You'll find this guy. Hey, remember that mobile meth lab you busted last year?

Jessica grinned in recollection.

"Yeah I remember. Took over three months to find that Winnebago. Bastards kept hiding in Horseheads."

"You found 'em though." Walter said while sipping his coffee.

"I got a lucky break." Jessica admitted. "I was just driving to clear my head and saw the smoke from an accident they had. Idiots about blew themselves to bits. Every one of 'em had to get cleared from Arnot Hospital before we could take 'em into custody."

Walter chuckled.

"Well, maybe you'll get another lucky break. Sometimes you just gotta wait."

"Thanks Walter." Jessica said with a smile.

"Detective! Detective Devins!" a woman's voice suddenly called out with urgency. Turning,

Jessica spotted a female officer rushing toward her. "What is it Rachael?" she asked as Officer Rachel Dawson handed her a piece of paper. "We just got phone call placing an anonymous tip. Two boys are near the library with a controlled substance as we speak. The caller claimed he saw them get it at a house at that address."

Jessica examined the paper with a frown.

"That's on Southside."

"It's also a lucky break." Walter said with a grin."

"A much needed one." Jessica added. "I've already put in for a warrant to search that house." Rachael said.

"Alright." Jessica started while moving toward the exit. "Walter, go catch up with those kids if you would. I'm gonna check out that house." As Jessica rushed on, the eyes of another officer watched her from his desk. Picking up his phone, he quickly made a phone call. With the receiver to his ear, he waited for his call to be answered. His eyes remained on Jessica, his observance going unnoticed as she vanished through the precinct's door.

"Hello?" a man's voice suddenly answered on the other end.

"Hey Kane, its Mitchel. We got a problem..."

Jessica slowly crept up to the house. Ducking beneath the railing of the front porch, she peered at the numbers on the mailbox that was in the front yard.

207... This is the place...

Tossing a glace back down the street, she calmed any fears that she might be spotted before proceeding with her investigations. Lights on within the dwelling and the sound of movement inside was clear enough indication that people were inside, giving Jessica reason to be cautious in her movements. Ducking beneath a series of windows, she made her way toward the back of the house. Reaching the back yard, she peeked around the corner of the house to spot several black trash bags piled up against the wall.

Checking her position again, Jessica moved closer to check the discarded refuse. Holes of varying size had been torn in many of the bags, leading her her deduce that they had been here long enough to be at the mercy of stray cats or other scavengers. Extracting a pair of latex gloves from an inside pocket of her denim jacket, she knelt over a bag and began sifting through the contents. Finding an empty antifreeze container, along with several empty pill packages, she frowned as she scanned over the list of ingredients on the back of the package.

Ephedrine. This has to be a meth house!

Suddenly, Jessica felt something hard jam against the back of her head, her heart sinking as she heard the familiar sound of a revolver's hammer being pulled back. Caught in a vulnerable position, she dared not make any sudden moves as a man's voice spoke.

"Hello Detective."

The startled youths took off in a panic at the arrival of the police squad car, bolting from behind the public library as the plump black office behind the wheel drove after them in pursuit. None payed the vagrant who watched events unfold from down the street any mind.

Clayton grinned wryly, having found a sense of amusement in what his handy work had wrought. Turning from the scene, he broke into a sprint once the area had cleared. He hoped that police would be equally responsive in checking out the address that he had provided with a simple anonymous tip. Still, he felt his efforts for the night were far from finished, and that he should, that he needed, to see things through to their conclusion.

忍

The florescent lights in the basement's ceiling served well in lighting the area. Stacked wooden crates and cardboard boxes of assorted size were clearly revealed as they sat about the walls of slate gray concrete. A trio of long tables spanned the length of one wall, their surfaces littered with an assortment of beakers, jugs of household chemicals, measuring cups, funnels, blenders, and Bunsen burners

Leaning against one of the support beams of the basement's ceiling, Jessica sat on the concrete floor. Tightly bound and gagged with duct tape, her face contorted in exertion as she struggled to free her hands and feet. The white soles of her dark blue sneakers scuffed the concrete as she pulled her knees up to her chest. A few strands of her hair fell across her face as she writhed in discomfort. An exhausted gasp leaked through the strip of tape that covered her mouth as she leaned her head back at fatigue's command.

A slight shiver coursed through her as the chilly air of her confines managed to seep through her dark blue sweatshirt and denim jacket. A numbing ache had begun to creep through her extremities. Her eyebrows sloped into a determined furrow as she locked her gaze on the cluttered tables along the wall across from her. Knowing it full well to be a meth lab, an anger burned inside of her, fueling a renewal of her struggles as she checked herself again.

I've got to find a way to free myself!

Not yet ready to surrender to her imprisonment, Jessica began searching her surroundings; her eyes suddenly gleaming with a new found hope as they came to rest on the floor at the end of the table. Barely able to move, she once more fought against the tape. Renewed purpose spurred her on as she dropped onto her side. Twisting herself about, she began scooting her way across the floor.

Muffled grunts escaped her gag with each movement as she inched along at a snail's pace. Eternity seemed to pass as she struggled on, her determined gaze fixed on a few shards of broken glass that lay scattered about underneath one of the tables. Exhaustion threatened to stop her. She knew she couldn't give up though. She could use the glass to cut her bonds, if she could only maneuver herself close enough to get to it. It was the only chance she had to escape. She *had* to make it.

Just a little further...

"I still say you're fuckin cheatin..."

"Fine, you deal then prick..."

"Asshole..."

The cards created a sharp rip as the man shuffled and broke the deck. With repetitive flicks of his wrist, he divided the cards face down amongst himself and three other gruff looking men who sat with him at the round kitchen table, its surface littered with beer bottles and smoking ash trays. Scooting back the wooden chair that was his seat, one of the men stood. Claiming a 9 mm hand gun from the table in front of him, he tucked its barrel into the front of his pants. "I still say we just take care of the little lady now and get rid of her body." he insisted as he seemed anxious to head through the door at his back.

"Would you just relax for fuck's sake?!" another of the men replied, glancing up from his hand while collecting more cards from the dealer. "She ain't goin nowhere, and Mister Kane will be here soon. When they get here we'll find out what the bitch knows and take care of her from there, like Mister Kane said."

"Think anyone knows she's here?" the card dealer asked.

"I'm sure The Medicine Man's inside people took care of it. We'd be up to our ass in 'bacon' if they hadn't. Just deal the cards already."

All in the kitchen turned toward the front door as it suddenly opened. A tall, dark haired man in a black suit and tie strode through. Neatly groomed, a long scar ran vertically down his right cheek, marring his otherwise immaculate appearance.

"Mister Kane."

Stopping, Robert Kane adjusted his black tie.

"Gentleman." he started. "I understand that we have a situation here, a detective Jessica Devins has dropped by for a little visit?"

The men all nodded in agreement.

"We got her down there." the man near the basement door volunteered with a casual gesture.

"Excellent." Kane said. "Bring her on up. We'll find out just how much she and her department knows about our operations."

The man turned toward the basement door, his boots creating heavy thumps upon the white tile of the floor. At the door's opening, a slender right hand suddenly shot out from its other side, swiftly jerking the pistol from the man's jeans. A left hand immediately followed to smash into his nose with an open palm. Blood gushed from the broken proboscis as he staggered backwards, the other three men at the table jumping up in alarm at the sudden commotion.

Jessica leaped through the open door. Landing upon her left foot, her right leg lashed out with a powerful front kick. The ball of her foot struck the man's chin, causing his head to snap back. A thin stream of blood trailed through the air. A single dislodged tooth flew from the man's mouth as he crashed to the floor.

With lightning reflexes, Jessica turned her newly acquired firearm on those seated at the table as the men fumbled for their own. "Freeze!" she ordered. Kane casually side stepped behind the cover of the doorway through which he had originally entered as the men managed to finally ready their weapons.

Ducking with hopes to avoid getting shot, Jessica strafed to her left while firing her pistol. Two more of the men fell to the floor, each taking a hit in the shoulder. The third managed to stumble back out of the kitchen and through the doorway.

Thinking quickly, Jessica dove for the kitchen table. Flipping it onto its side, she managed to duck behind it as the last of the men emerged from his cover once more. She knew the table wouldn't be the best cover in a fire fight, but it was the only thing available. Moving and shooting simultaneously, the man strode back into the kitchen while trying to track his target's movement. Three shots ripped holes in the kitchen's dry wall and cabinets at Jessica's rear. A fourth tore through the tabletop's surface. Jessica's eyes widened in horror as her cover was pierced, the wood of the table's underside splintering mere inches from her face.

Holy shit!

忍

The gunshots from within the house blasted the chilly night air as Robert Kane emerged from the house's front door. Making his way down the steps of the porch, he pulled a cell phone from his pocket as he began making his way across its front yard toward a white Jeep Cherokee parked nearby. Briefly taking his eyes off of his vehicle, he dialed a number and placed the phone to his ear as he continued on.

Detective Devins' escape from capture was an incident that he hadn't anticipated. It was his hope that she would be killed in the shootout which now transpired behind him. He knew the place would be crawling with cops soon though, and he'd need to be far from the reach of the Elmira Police Department.

Suddenly, a hand shot across Kane's face from behind. His eyes widened in surprise as it covered his mouth and hooked underneath his nose, pain shooting through it as his head was pulled back. The cell phone fell from his grasp as he felt a foot stamp into the back of his knee to further break his balance. A second hand quickly snaked around, placing an open palm under his chin. His arms flailed helplessly as he was swiftly taken off of his feet, the air rushing from his lungs as he landed hard on his back. With no time to react to what was happening, blackness soon followed as a fist descended to strike with a hammer blow.

Clayton stood, looking down at the now unconscious Kane, glancing to the cell phone that lay in the grass nearby as a woman's voice answered the number that Kane had dialed before being ambushed.

"U.S. Airlines, how may we help you?"

Clayton tuned back to Kane.

"My apologies, it would seem your flight has been canceled."

The sound of approaching police sirens snagged his attention. The gunfire inside had ceased, and he knew he could not be seen here. The police could handle things from here. Leaving Kane to lay in the front lawn, Clayton dashed off to disappear into the night.

忍

Thinking quickly, Jessica shoved against the table's underside, easily sliding it across the tile of the kitchen floor. The advancing gunman halted his advance to catch himself, nearly tripping over the piece of furniture in his hurried movement. Leaping up to her feet, Jessica lashed out with a side kick. The heel of her foot smashed into the man's sternum, sending him sprawling to the floor across from her as the pistol flew from his grasp.

A chorus of agonized groans rose from the floor as the wail of sirens heralded the arrival of police backup. Breathing heavily, Jessica looked around at the injured men who lay scattered about.

"You're all under arrest."

A smile of accomplishment spanned Jessica's face as she gathered her things from her desk. Slipping her arms into the sleeves of her jacket in preparation for her departure from the precinct, she looked up to see Walter approaching.

"Great collar you made tonight, Detective." he complimented with his usual grin.

"Thanks." she replied while collecting her car keys and case file. "How did things go with those two kids?"

Walter chuckled.

"Well, after seeing their parent's reaction, I'd bet they would rather go to jail."

"Yeah I bet." Jessica smirked before bringing seriousness back to the topic of discussion. "What about Kane? Any idea why he was laying out in the front yard?"

"He claims someone jumped him outside." Rachael suddenly answered as she strolled over to join the conversation. "Never even saw his attacker from what he says. Wants to press assault charges though."

"Sure, we'll get right on that arrest warrant for the invisible man." Walter joked again before turning to Jessica. "Gotta love the good Samaritan, eh Detective?"

Jessica smirked.

"You guys have a good night."

"Take care Jessica." Rachael said.

Walter waved farewell as Jessica made her way to the exit.

"Good night Detective."

Police chief William Higgins strode calmly through the busy restaurant. Appareled in brown suit with a black tie, the other finely dressed patrons paid him no mind as he moved amid their dining experience. Stopping before a table at the back, he addressed a lone man who was seated there; his appearance hidden behind an upraised menu.

"Mister Sinclair..."

Dark, neatly combed hair with gray streaks peeked over the menu's top as it lowered to reveal an aged man in a white Armani suit.

"Chief Higgins." Rolland Sinclair said as he closed the menu and placed it on the table. With a wrinkling hand, he gestured toward the seat across from him.

"Please."

Pulling out the chair, Higgins seated himself. "I understand that you wished to see me regarding a problem." Sinclair continued while sipping at a glass of red wine.

"Yes." Higgins said. "It's Detective Devins. She is getting dangerously close to your operation."

Sinclair stared into the long stemmed wine glass in quiet reflection.

"Devins." he finally said after a brief pause. "It has been some time since that name has come to my attention..." He remembered well the night that he claimed the life of Officer Robert Devins. He was much younger then, and had yet to adapt the identity of The Medicine Man.

As a leading supplier at the time, he hadn't expected a police raid when he was meeting at an abandoned warehouse with some of his top dealers. He narrowly escaped the shootout to follow as he managed to find his way through a back exit. Devins followed, aided with cover fire from fellow officers.

If the Devil did indeed look after his own, Sinclair's survival on that night was proof enough as Devins somehow twisted his ankle in the ensuing chase through Elmira's alleyways. Sinclair could have ran on to escape the police, but the persistent officer had possibly seen his face. Going back to finish the fallen policeman, Sinclair shot him in the back with a small caliber pistol before fleeing into the night.

Going into hiding, he managed to purchase several local businesses with the ill-gotten wealth he had amassed. The companies under his auspice flourished as he would return to his criminal ways years later. Never again would he make the mistake of operating publicly however, as he would conduct his business through the use of front men and police corruption. Thus, The Medicine Man was born.

Sinclair turned his gaze back to Chief Higgins as his thoughts returned to the present. "Devins arrested Kane two nights ago." Higgins continued.

"Yes, I saw that on the news."Sinclair said with a rough sigh. That is most unfortunate..."

"He is planning to volunteer information on you in exchange for immunity." Higgins continued.

Seemingly unfazed by this news, Sinclair grinned as he took another sip of wine.

"Well, we shall have to do something about that, won't we?"

Sinclair looked up as a waiter in black approached. "Are you ready to order, sir?" he asked politely.

Sinclair smiled.

"Yes, I believe I am."

Unexpected Death Hinders Medicine Man Investigation.
By Clayton Drake

Elmira NY- Authorities efforts to apprehend the drug lord known only as The Medicine Man were dealt a serious blow, with the sudden death of Robert Kane. Kane, who was arrested for possession and distribution of an illegal substance, was found dead during the early hours of the morning in his cell at the Elmira Police Department. Sources estimate the time of death was between 1 and 3 am. According to sources in the Elmira P.D., Kane had information which was vital to The Medicine Man's operations. A coroner declared a stroke to be the cause of death, with no further comments being offered by the department.

Moonlight poured through the window of the otherwise dark bed room, shining upon the newspaper as it lay on the table before it. Clayton's heart ached as he gazed down at the article on its front page, having written it just one day ago. Gloved in black, his hands rose as he placed the palms over his face and ran them down to clasp together at his chin. Protective armored sleeves covered the back of the hands and forearms as his form was garbed in a black V-neck jacket and matching trousers. Placing both hands on the table's surface for support, he leaned on it while lifting his gaze to the window. Seconds passed as he stared out into the night in silent contemplation.

The Medicine Man, the man responsible for Randy's death, was still out there. He had hoped that simply lending aid to local law enforcement would be enough to bring him down. The mysterious drug lord worked from the shadows just as he did however, and he now knew he would have to do a lot more to destroy his empire.

Turning his gaze back to the table's surface, he claimed a black hood from atop it. The three guiding principles of his training began to echo in his mind as he slipped the hood over his head.

To hide is defense...

His eyes narrowed in the dark from behind the mask that covered his mouth and nose as he looked over several thin flat plates of metal that lay before him. With a hole in their centers, their points numbered four as he began collecting them in one hand while stacking them in the other. Mindful of the razor sharp edges of the shuriken throwing blades, he tucked the stack of nine into the folds of the jacket as he eyed a length of chain that also lay on the table; each end of it bearing a heavy ball weight.

Violence is to be avoided...

He knew combat to be an inevitability however, in spite of any peaceful intentions that he had, and he would have to be prepared to engage in such. Claiming the Kusari Fundo fighting chain, he tucked it into a black sash that was around his waist.

Use of the sword is for peace, and to protect family, country, and nature...

Clayton turned from the table, his stride silent and graceful as the carpet caressed the soles of the soft split toed boots that he wore. Stepping from his house into the cool night air, he stared at the city lights off in the distance. He had found his way into The Medicine Man's world before, and he was certain that he could do so again. The very shadows from which the drug lord ruled would soon turn against him, serving as an armor that even his best guns would be useless against. He would come to know and fear a foe that he could not see, and the power which that foe possessed; the power of the Ninja.

Jessica placed two plastic grocery bags and a gallon of milk on top of her kitchen counter. Opening the nearby refrigerator, she placed the milk inside along with a carton of eggs that she extracted from one of the bags. With her perishables taken care of, she left her kitchen area as she decided to hold off on the putting away of her remaining groceries til later.

Making her way past her sofa and coffee table, she stopped at her living room window. Staring out into the moon lit night beyond, she thought back on Robert Kane's arrest. As one of The Medicine Man's top suppliers, he had been a solid lead on the drug lord's operations. He had been in custody but for a few days, and was planning to trade immunity for vital information and testimony in a court of law. Then death took him from her, a coroner proclaiming a sudden stroke to be the cause of his demise. She was back in the dark again, with no leads as to the identity of The Medicine Man, and no one to blame for her failures but death.

Releasing a sigh of emotional exhaustion, Jessica closed the curtains to the window and turned away from it as she pondered what to do that would bring The Medicine Man to justice. Facing the comfort of her sofa, her eyes came to rest on a framed photo of her with her father that sat upright on an end table at the couch's side.

She wished that he was there to offer counsel or encouragement. He was gone however, one more thing death had taken from her.

Jessica frowned in her thoughts.

I'm so tired of death...

忍

"A pleasure doin business with ya."

Thomas Lesco stepped back from the passenger side of the tan, rusted Buick Park Avenue as its window rolled back up. Smiling to himself, he watched as the vehicle drove off.

Well, that was an easy two hundred bucks.

Placing the roll of bills into the pocket of a rough looking brown leather coat, he turned to head on across the street.

Next stop, Sutherton Park...

With his hands in his coat pockets, he strolled casually along toward his intended destination. Unseen on the rooftops above him, a shadowy figure crouched while watching his movement. From his vantage point above the city's streets, Clayton's eyes narrowed with a determined stare from behind the dark mask that covered his visage.

So it begins...

www.ingramcontent.com/pod-product-compliance
Lightning Source LLC
Chambersburg PA
CBHW021043130626
46552CB00005B/1990